The Stone Men

The
Stone Men

MURRAY HERBERT

For Anne, Cameron, Douglas and Catriona,
who believed in the Stone Men
from the very beginning

First published 2001
by House of Lochar

A CIP catalogue record for this book
is available from the British Library.

ISBN 1 899863 79 6

Typeset in Plantin Light by XL Publishing Services, Tiverton
Printed in Great Britain
by SRP Ltd, Exeter
for House of Lochar
Isle of Colonsay, Argyll PA61 7YR

Contents

About This Tale

This story came to me on one of those long summer nights of my childhood as I sat in Kirsten's small, neat house, listening as she told me tales about life on the croft when she had been young. The day had been long and hot, and I was tired after a lengthy hike in search of good fishing. Now as the darkness outside deepened, and the moths darted and flapped noisily round the dim lights, I was complaining loudly about having to pay to fish the lochs up at Moidart for trout.

'Who do they think they are,' I moaned, 'living away in the south and thinking they own the fish in the water? They hardly own the land and *they* didn't put the fish in them, did they? How can they call it *their* land? It belongs to those who live on it, not those who think they own it!'

Kirsten gazed long into the fire, deep in thought, and then spoke, quietly.

'Whose indeed, Murray? We have the land for such a short while, but whose was it in the beginning?' Her voice trailed off and she seemed lost in her thoughts once more. I sat quiet and waited, she would soon carry on.

Then came this story, which she told hesitantly and reluctantly, half fearful it seemed, that I would not believe her. In fact she was quite right, for I could not bring myself to accept her account at all, and dismissed it as no more than a highland legend – rather like one of the fairy tales of the little folk which my grandmother had often told to amuse me when I was very young. It was so unlike any of the stories Kirsten had ever told me before, about the people who once had lived and farmed in the area. I had never before doubted any of the things that

Kirsten had spoken of, for I had often heard them told by other folk in the village. But this story was different and I confess was so strange, that I rejected it. In time I quite forgot it – or so I thought.

It was only last year, some dozen or so since Kirsten herself had died, that I had a curious experience, near Glendrian. This woke in me a memory of Kirsten, old and wizened, cradling her gnarled hands on her lap and gazing intently into the dying embers of a fire as she told me this tale of a summer some eighty or so years earlier. The story came back to me in snatches through the mist of years and sent me plodding in search of other landmarks of her tale. Some I could still identify, but others have now passed and will never be seen again. I was not, however, prepared for my final discovery.

There had never really been any cause to disbelieve her, for she was as honest as the day. I only wish I had had the opportunity to tell her what I had found.

Chapter 1

The Footprints in the Sand

For two hours she had waited, pinching herself to stay awake, until she was sure by the steady breathing of the others in the room that it was safe to move. Now, very cautiously, the girl slipped her feet out from under the blankets and swung her legs onto the floor. The glow of a dying fire in the grate gave just enough light for her to see Hughie on his bed, in one corner of the room. Her parents were asleep behind a screen and her grandmother in a small recess beside the fireplace. Very carefully, she gathered her shawl and shoes in her arms and made her way silently across the floor.

At the door she paused for a moment, fearful of any noise that would disturb them, and then quickly lifted the latch. The door swung gently open letting out the quietest of creaks. From behind the screen, came the sound of her father rolling over, muttering something in his sleep. Kirsten held her breath, not daring to move, fearing discovery.

After some minutes, when she was once more sure that it was safe to proceed, she quickly twisted herself round the half open door, shut it behind her and waited on the threshold, her heart pounding. That part of the journey was accomplished, at least.

Now she moved on through the narrow gap between the croft houses, taking care not to disturb McKinnon's dogs, until she had reached the edge of the small hamlet. The light of a nearly full moon was enough for her to see her way down to the edge of the gurgling burn where very gingerly, she set out over the stepping stones, taking careful, calculated steps, until she had safely reached the other bank. From here the journey was easier, for the path was so well known to her that she could have journeyed it blindfold. The bay was less than half a mile off and Kirsten reckoned she could be back at the house in an hour if she hurried and had no difficulty in her search. There would be trouble if she failed, and the one thing Kirsten did not want, was any more trouble. Of course it had been wrong to take the spyglass without asking Hughie, but she also knew that he would have refused. All she had wanted was to have a good look at the whale. What was the harm in that?

Soon the rough sheep track gave out and she stumbled on through the tufty, mossy edge of the bog until finally she was over the crest of the hill and could clamber over the rocks and down to a small sandy bay – the bay that she always thought of as *her* bay. The sea was quiet tonight, the air calm and still warm, and waves lapped gently, like a lullaby, on the shore. It was so peaceful and Kirsten, therefore, felt every hope that she would succeed in her task. Quietly and quickly she worked her way round to the small headland that formed the farther edge of the little bay.

This was the spot where she had sat for an hour that afternoon, watching the whale, as it surfaced, its back arching, blowing noisily and playing off the shore. It had seemed so graceful – so free, and after a spell, she had paddled in the water to be nearer it. Now she reproached herself for if she had stayed on the rocks she might not have left the wretched thing behind. Hughie would certainly miss it in the morning if she did not find it. She had to find it.

Hopefully, she searched first the surface, and then the crannies of the rocks for just a glint in the moonlight that would show her its metal casing. With mounting despair she found none, and as it dawned on her that she must have left the spyglass below the high-water line, she began to feel sick and helpless. With its cork waist it was designed to float, so surely by now, it must have been washed off the rocks by the receding tide and far out into deeper water. She felt utterly hopeless and stood gazing out over the sea, straining to find any sign of it bobbing on the water.

Suddenly Kirsten had the distinct impression that she was not alone on the beach. Instinctively she ducked down behind a rock and listened very acutely for any sound. Could she have been followed? Something in her wanted to stay well out of sight and remain undiscovered. It would not do to be found on the beach at this time of night.

A noise drifted across the quiet bay – a noise she could not quite identify – a kind of grumbling, growling sound that Kirsten did not like. She flattened herself against the rock and waited, heart pounding, for several long minutes. It did not sound like a man. Once more she thought she heard a grunt or growl a little further off but then, only the sound of the sea rippling upon the sand. Slowly she lifted her head and reconnoitred. The bay was empty. Very carefully she drew herself out from the protection of the rocks and began to retrace her steps.

The moon, now half hidden behind a bank of wispy cloud which was drawing up from the west, gave just enough light for her to see her way from the small headland to the beach. At the higher reaches of this, the deeper shadow showed where the sand gave way once more to stone and boulders.

She was walking slowly, picking her route carefully in the dim light, her eyes fixed on the ground, trying to stick to the runs of wet sand between the rocks and to avoid stumbling. As she moved on she became aware of some kind of depression in the sand, just ahead of her.

Approaching cautiously, she fell to her knees and gently placed her hand in the mark. It was fresh, wet where the surface sand had been forced aside, and seemed to her to be quite wide, bigger than her hand. Kirsten was puzzled. She had not come across this part of the beach on her way to the headland. A feeling of unease filled her and she glanced up, half in panic. Faintly, some distance off, she fancied a muffled sound once more, though she could not be certain. Maybe she was imagining it – perhaps it was a cow or a sheep on the hill. Noise carries far at night, especially on such a still night as this and close to the water. But this noise was somehow strange and Kirsten did not like it.

Then, just for a few moments, the moon broke free through a hole in the cloud casting a clear, pale shaft of light across the hillside. On the skyline, about half a mile off, there was a movement. It was too far away to make out what it was, merely a dark shadow on the hill top, moving, and in that fleeting moment Kirsten's heart stood still.

Frantically, she scrambled to her feet and ran as fast as she could over the rocks to the path at the back of the bay. It was difficult, for the moon was now dimmed again behind thicker cloud, and in the half dark, she fell two or three times bruising her shins and cutting her arm. She fled up the small hill and across the boggy moor towards the village. Her legs ached as she ran and her breath came in burning gasps, until she felt she could run no further. It was only when she had crossed the burn once more that she dared to stop and draw her breath.

Here, among the familiar cottages she felt safe again and at the same time, quite stupid. She called herself a fool for being frightened by an animal. It must have been a deer straying down to the shore – they often did at this time of year, or perhaps one of the cows. Yes, she was quite sure of it now – a deer or a cow. Her imagination was too vivid – wasn't her mother always telling her so?

Outside the door of her home, she paused until her panting breath eased, then silently stole back into the croft house. The fire had now burnt out, but where the moon shone in through the window she could still make out Hughie's figure sprawled on his bed, his position unchanged from when she had left. Everything was completely still and safe. There was no spyglass to place on the floor next to Hughie's boots as she had hoped – she would have to face up to that problem in the morning. For now, she was very tired and crept back under her covers. The fear she had felt on the beach faded into a mist now that she was among the familiar smells of her home, and fatigue overcame her. Soon the rhythmic breathing of her family in the small house lulled her to sleep, and for all her problems it was a deep sleep she kept until morning.

Kirsten was standing with her eyes cast down at the floor trying to avoid her mother's gaze. The lecture had been going on all morning since Hughie had made the discovery and a confession had been wrung out of the girl. At first, she had tried to deny it outright, but she was not a good liar and her mother instinctively knew the truth. Now she was reaping the consequences of her deceit.

'I cannot believe that you did such a wicked thing, Kirsten,' her mother was saying again. 'You are a wicked, thankless girl. Full of lies.'

'But all I wanted to do was to look at the whale better, mother,' she said limply. There was little more that could be added. Hughie had been livid and stormed off to see to the cow. Her father looked hurt at her half-hearted untruth, and her mother had spent all morning forcing her to all manner of tasks around the home, punishing her with work and the sharp edge of her tongue. 'But why can't I go now, mother? Please, please let me,' begged the girl.

'Simply because I am telling you to find your father first!' snapped her mother in reply. 'You will have to wait until later to go back to the bay. Now, will you go down to the boats, now that I am asking you, and ask your father to bring some kindling home, when he comes?' The woman stood up straight, wiped her hands on her apron and looked sternly at her daughter. 'I need it, and plenty of it, in time for making the lunch. And you will stay and help him gather it, mind!' She swung round abruptly, indicating that the matter was closed and returned to sifting flour into a basin.

'But, mother…' Kirsten began. There was silence. She sighed. Kirsten knew when to stop. 'Very well, I'll go then,' she said sulkily.

Leaving the house, she set off out of the village in a dark mood. Why did every thing seem to go against her? All morning her mother had been shouting at her. It wasn't even as if it had really been her fault. Still, she had not dared to tell her about her trip to the bay in the dark. (Nor would she.) That would have to remain a secret – they were angry enough already.

She looked at the sun. By now the tide would be coming in. Maybe, just maybe, the spyglass would have been washed up on the tide – even though her father had pointed out that the tide runs out at that edge of the bay, far beyond the Point itself. Hughie, of course, reckoned that it would by now be in the mid Atlantic. If only it could be found, they might forgive her.

But now here she was, forced to take a detour down to the larger village of Sanna, half a mile off down the stream. Her father would be there for some time yet as it was still some hours before lunch.

Kirsten began to argue with herself. Surely, there would be enough time to run over to the beach first on the way. It would not take long. They would never know. And so the girl turned her path to the side, and set off on her detour, choosing the hope of finding the glass before the orders of her angry mother.

It was a hot morning and Kirsten was tired after the excursion of the previous night. Therefore, once at the top of the small hill above the village, she threw herself down for a rest on the soft springy grass and stared, for a time, out to sea.

The air was crystal clear, like polished glass. Out to the north-west she could see as far even as the Uists. Beyond them, she knew, the restless miles of the Atlantic stretched on to the Americas, but to Kirsten those islands stood like watchers on the very edge of the World. Lying between her and these outposts, the nearer islands of Canna, Rum, Eigg and Muck sailed like ships in a steady ocean, and to the north the jagged outline of Skye stood like the ramparts of a great castle. Behind her lay her little hamlet of Plocaig, nothing more than a cluster of small, thatched and whitewashed croft houses set in a dry island of turf, in the centre of the peat bog. It clung close to the small, winding, brown stream she had crossed the previous night. She had her secret spots along this burn, where she would guddle for the small trout that darted from the shadows of the heathery bank to hide under boulders and small clumps of reeds, or where she studied the dragon flies as they buzzed over the pools.

Downstream, Sanna rested among its sand dunes and under the craggy hills that dominated the skyline. This was her world, the islands, the hills and the few small villages, all very safe, secure and unchanging. But it was the bay that was her favourite spot – her bay. Here she went to collect driftwood, or fish, or think, or dream. Few of the other villagers ever went there, unless a stray sheep or an adventurous cow had wandered down onto the beach. But Kirsten escaped there whenever she could.

Her mother's anger still made her smart inside. They never understood her. She drew herself back from her thoughts and rose to continue on to the beach.

Soon she had crested the last small hill, just as she had done in the dark some hours earlier, and stopped. Below her lay the bay, a half cup of silver-white sand about a hundred yards wide, carved out between two rocky outcrops. You could not see it until you were almost upon it and it was this seclusion that delighted Kirsten most. The farthest of the promontories sheltered it from the roughest seas making it a relatively calm spot unless the tide and wind were running from the north west. At its higher reaches the sand was lost under shingle and the boulders and irregular rocks, she had found so difficult in the dark.

Taking a deep breath she trotted down a track to the sand. It was still calm and the high full moon tide was about an hour from its highest point. For some time she searched meticulously all over the rocks but soon her worst fears were confirmed, for there was no sight or trace of the spyglass to be found. Then, on retracing her steps to leave the bay, she suddenly stopped dead, staring.

There were the impressions that she had seen the night before. She had almost forgotten them and at first thought she must have made them herself. But surely she had not ventured this far along the beach in the dark. They were not the ordinary prints of a deer, if indeed they were prints at all. They were quite unlike anything that she had ever seen before, not those of any of animal she knew, or for that matter, of a man. She fell onto her knees and examined them keenly. Already the damp sand was drying out and they were beginning to fill in, as wisps of light, dry sand blew into the imprints.

There was a repeating pattern. A large padded imprint like the footwork of a giant dog – much larger than that of a cow, or a horse, a little larger even than her own foot which she gently tested in the mark. It was, in general shape, rounder than her own and had a clear padded effect, not unlike that of a dog or a fox, she decided. To the left of these marks (if you considered the general direction in which they appeared to be travelling) the sand was scored with regular shallow furrows, about two feet long and running in the same direction as the paw prints. At one end of these the sand was twisted into a ragged shallow bowl.

As she bent forward and studied them with a knitted brow her hand closed on a stone half buried in the sand. It fitted neatly into her hand and she picked it up. The stone was around the size and shape of an egg, but with one flattened end. It was quite regular, which was unusual in itself, had a bluish tinge and was opaque like dull glass, rather than solid in colour. It had a slightly roughened surface and seemed at a casual glance to have a circular line running near one end. Kirsten liked the feel of it in her hand, and rolled it over and over in her palm as she puzzled over the peculiar indentations that the feet of this animal had made. She was perplexed and now followed the track along the shore until, to her dismay, it was lost in the rising sea. The memory of the fear that she had inexplicably felt the previous night came back to her, although in the bright, warm sunshine she was now merely confused, not afraid.

Kirsten sat down on a rock near the water's edge, her chin cupped in one hand, rolling the stone over and over again in the other, deep in thought. What kind of animal could have made these markings? What was the noise she had heard? And so she sat puzzled for a long time completely forgetting her errand and her family, until suddenly she was roused by an exasperated hail from the rocky hilltop above the bay. 'Kirst-en!' She looked up and saw Hughie descending with large strides, fury in his eyes.

'What on earth are you doing now?' he demanded when he reached his sister. 'First my spyglass…'

'Oh, Hughie, I'm sorry,' sobbed the girl, 'I only came back to look for it.' She looked pleadingly at him and he saw that she was indeed upset.

Still he persisted, '…and now Mother is as angry as a crab with you. The fire's not yet lit, father's wanting his food and so am I. Come on!' He was very angry indeed and grabbing the stone from her tossed it among the shale and boulders. 'What are you doing now anyway?'

'Just thinking, Hughie,' she answered tearfully, but attempting the disarming smile she usually used to avert her family's anger or frustration with her.

'About what?'

'Just those marks in the sand.'

'What marks are you talking about, Kirsten?'

'Those ones there,' she said, motioning with her arm to the waters edge. But the tide had risen and now covered every inch of the trail she had followed. The traces had been swallowed up in the sea. Everything in the bay was as normal and peaceful as it had been for hundreds of thousands of years.

Chapter 2

The Second Sighting

The journey back to the crofthouse passed too quickly for Kirsten. All the while she was anticipating the rough edge of her mother's tongue and wished Hughie would slow down. Somehow she would have to try and deflect her mother's anger again.

As they finally drew near to the village her pace slowed further and she dropped a yard or two behind her brother, unhappy and unsure. Their home was at the farthest end of the huddle of squat houses. A few sheep and chickens idled in the narrow gap that pretended to be a short street, and scattered as the two waded through them. She hung back still further. Her mother had, she realised, every right to be extremely angry with her. Better to get it over with. She took a deep breath and plunged in through the low doorway.

It was confusing and surprising, therefore, to find her mother beaming on her appearance.

'Here's the wee absent-minded lassie at last,' she said laughingly, her soft voice sounding like a wind blowing gently on the trees. 'Head full of nonsense and never able to remember a thing at all, Sandy.'

Sandy? Kirsten swung round and saw sitting on a low wooden chair by the cold and empty fireplace, the reason for her mother's strangely forgiving mood.

'Uncle Sandy!' She squealed and threw herself across the room into his arms. Her mother could never be angry when her brother was home. He brought a calm to their house and a cheer like a warm fire on an icy night. 'I

19

didn't know you were coming. When did you get here?'

'Och it would be about, let me see,' he made a great play of taking an old time piece from his waistcoat pocket and examining it in the dim light of the room, 'about a whole hour ago. And do you know, Kirsten,' he continued with a gleam in his eye, 'I am still waiting for a cup of tea? Highland hospitality! They say that there's a shortage of wood for the fires in Plocaig these days. Here's me travelled twice round the world since I last set foot on Ardnamurchan and I can't even get a drop of hot water. Something about poor service from the carriers, I hear. That's a lame excuse I say.'

He winked at his sister who shook her head, sighed and set about rectifying the absence of warmth and hot food and drink within the crofthouse. Kirsten was doubly glad to see her uncle. There was no question but that he had saved her from further, just punishment that afternoon.

Hughie was sent off to fetch some peat from the stack outside, and his father to collect some potatoes and kail from the croft. Her father's ancient mother, who had lived with them since she had been widowed, had been dozing quietly in the corner and now began to rouse from sleep, listening with interest to the conversation. An air of busyness settled on the little house. Sandy, however, sat back in his chair and regarded Kirsten with his keen eyes.

'My but you have grown since I last saw you, Kirsten. You look more like your mother every day with those grey eyes and the red just showing into your hair. You'll be a fine woman just like her one day. Ah Jessie, you should be really proud of her.'

Kirsten stood back and took in his face. Nothing ever seemed to change in Sandy. His eyes sparkled deep blue, like the sea itself. There was something wild and adventurous in them, something that echoed in her heart.

She longed to roam the oceans and travel to new worlds like him. Yet, despite all the adventures and troubles they had seen his eyes remained homely and kind. He was a short stocky man, hewn as it were from the very rock of Ardnamurchan, with a broad, bushy beard, now greying round the edges. His face and big hands were burned brown by the sun and the sea air, and when he walked it was with the rolling gait of one accustomed to the heave of the sea under his legs.

'Uncle Sandy, how long are you here for?'

'That depends. My ship's in Glasgow for repairs and we won't be sailing again until October. Though some of my crew have been sent off on another ship they let the captain wait for his own vessel. So here I am with the best folk on all God's earth.'

'Till October?' said Kirsten with delight.

'Aye.'

'Aye, aye sir!' she cried, beaming.

'It's a shame we can't be putting you up here, Sandy,' observed Kirsten's father, as he re-entered.

'Never mind that, Jamie,' the other reassured him. 'I'll be staying down at Sanna with our mother. Ah it will be good to have the ground under my feet again. No matter where I have been on this earth my heart always comes back to Ardnamurchan. Believe me there is no better place to be and no better sight in the world than seeing the sun sinking in a clear sky out there over the Uists. I always see that sight in my mind, whether I'm off the Cape or Newfoundland.'

After an interval during which Sandy plied them with questions about the village, the stock, the crofts and every man, mawsie and bairn that he could remember, Kirsten's mother brought a bowl of broth, some bread and steaming tea and set it down on a small table at Grandmother's elbow. The rest of the family gathered round a larger table placed by a window set deep in the rough stonework of the house. Having given thanks they fell on their food, for the meal was later than usual and all were hungry.

The talk turned once more to livestock, the state of the fishing, and the general running of the croft.

'Ah! but we seem to be losing more of the stock these days,' began Kirsten's father.

'How so, Jamie?'

'I don't rightly know. They likely fall off the cliffs and are washed out into the sea. We never find any sign of them. McKinnon at Sanna lost a cow last month and they say over in Kilmory they lost two sheep in a week.'

'Good! I don't do with sheep,' exclaimed the old woman bitterly, from her corner. Her son cast her a glance of caution.

'You will have to see my ram, Uncle Sandy,' said Hughie enthusiastically. 'It's the best we've ever reared and bound to win at the show.'

'Aye, and who will be judging the show this year?' he enquired.

'There's just the two,' began his father. 'A lad from way up Lochailort way…'

'…and…and Alasdair McColl,' broke in Kirsten excitedly. She wanted to impress Sandy with her knowledge.

There was a commotion from the seat by the fireplace, where her grandmother appeared to choke on a piece of potato in her broth. She knocked over her bowl and shouted, 'McColl! A curse on their name. McColl! – never trust a McColl! That name is never to be spoken in our house, ever again. Do you hear?' She glowered savagely at Kirsten who felt the blood rush to her ears and cheeks. What was upsetting her grandmother so?

'Nana!' cautioned Kirsten's father, 'Never call a curse on anyone.'

'But McColl's…' she howled again.

'Not even McColls.'

The old lady clenched her wrinkled hands into tight fists and tears rose up in her eyes. 'It was all due to a McColl,' she sobbed.

'Now, now, Mother,' soothed her son, 'That's all by with now and Alasdair's not even related. He really is a very fine man – and a good judge of animals.' He cast a quick knowing glance at his wife and Sandy, and handed the old lady back her spoon which had fallen upon the floor.

Kirsten was upset and disconcerted by this outburst of her grandmother's. What was it that had caused her to react so violently? Who was this McColl and why was his name never to be spoken in their house? She had never heard it before and guessed that there was probably a good reason for it. She would ask Sandy one day, when she had the chance.

An uneasy silence settled over the family, and at length it was Sandy who broke the stillness, taking a sudden and genuine interest in the details of Hughie's ram.

Two weeks later, the clear, warm weeks of May had given way to a series of relentlessly wet and drizzly days such as can only be experienced on the coastlines of Scotland. Kirsten was heading off in the company of Hughie and Malcolm McKinnon, the only other child in Plocaig, on their daily trek to school. The journey took them three miles over the crags of *Meall Sanna* to Achoshnish village in the next valley. Every day of school year the trio made this journey, usually in silence.

This morning a hoary mist lay close about them, soft rain dripped down their necks and they could see no further than the length of the village. The air smelt peaty and heavy and the sound of the foghorn in Stevenson's lighthouse, on the Point, echoed from the hills around them, like the eerie bellow of a giant bull.

They were part way up on their ascent of *Meall Sanna* when Kirsten suddenly stopped and cried out in dismay. She had forgotten the peat Mr Shearer insisted they bring on such days and that would mean certain punishment from the master. Calling to the others to go on ahead she turned and bounded back down the hill as fast as the mist would allow, across the bog to collect one from the peat stack by her home. By the time she had retraced her steps and reached the hillside once more, she reckoned Hughie and Malcolm would be over the summit. If she pushed on she might yet overtake them and avoid the wrath of the teacher by arriving in time.

In the fog, and in her hurry, she must have strayed to one side or the other, for gradually she became aware that she no longer recognised the usual landmarks of the journey. She knew she was on the hillside above Sanna but whether the track lay to her left or to her right it was impossible to tell. The only course was to continue up, for she must eventually descend into the Achoshnish valley, from where she could follow the stream to the schoolhouse.

Suddenly Kirsten stopped dead in her tracks, her mouth falling open in amazement. Unmistakably in the soft peaty earth, where a clod of the hill had broken away leaving a small strip of flat soil, lay a single imprint; the image of the one she had seen on the beach, round with a padded mark, only – perhaps by a trick of the soft yellowish light – this one seemed larger. At first she was puzzled and looked nearby, in vain, for another print. The rest of the ground was too heathery or rocky; this was the only mark to be seen.

Quite suddenly she felt very alone and exposed on the hillside. In panic she pushed upwards until she had left the mark well behind. Presently, as she had planned, she cut across the stream and judged from its size that she ought to work upstream to the schoolhouse. By the time she arrived, wet and breathless, the lesson was well underway and Mr Shearer, dispelled any fears she had had about being alone on the hill by the example of his fury at her tardiness.

That afternoon the mist blew off and a pale, watery sun escaped from time to time from behind banks of hurrying white clouds. The air had a fresh clean feel unlike the dankness of the morning and the trio set off home in a happier mood. When they arrived, they found a state of excitement in Plocaig and Sanna. A gaggle of the crofters were gathered in a circle leaning on the rough walls and wooden spars of a sheep pen, deep in argument. The gate was lying open and the men did not notice Kirsten as she quietly sidled up to the group and squatted on a boulder near her father.

'No one would be doing such a thing, Archie,' he was saying.

'Well I don't know, Jamie, they are strange people over there running the Estate now. It's all I can think of.'

'But that's all of fourteen miles away – you're not telling me they came and took your beasts in the night.'

'I don't know, ever since McColl…'

'Shh!' hushed another, 'A curse on the McColls.'

'Enough of that, now,' cautioned Jamie, 'The Lord does not want us to be calling curses. It will come to no good.'

'All I'm saying is it's a terribly strange thing,' answered the other.

'Aye, I don't like it one little bit,' put in one of the MacPhails, from Sanna, 'There have been too many of the stock going missing altogether. It's uncanny, not at all right. I've never heard of such a thing before.'

'Are you right sure you shut the gate last night?' enquired his brother.

'As sure as I know you're standing here in front of me,' cried out the bereft crofter irritably.

Without thinking, from her spot on the boulder, Kirsten piped up abruptly, 'It could it have been an animal eating them.'

Silence descended on the group. This was an unwelcome intrusion to their serious discussion.

'Now don't you be daft, lass,' said old MacPhail, a round, wizened man who was the senior of the gathering. He had been standing listening intently, silently puffing on his pipe while the others had been talking, 'There's no chance of that,' he said. A chorus of chuckles rose from the group of men, and Hughie who had, like Kirsten, taken up an unobtrusive position in the circle, joined in heartily.

Kirsten felt the colour rise in her cheeks. 'But I saw a huge footprint on *Meall Sanna* this morning,' she protested and then added with sudden inspiration. '– like a wolf's.' The chorus of chuckles swelled into a wave of laughter.

'Now, Kirsten,' warned her father, 'don't you be telling your tales again.'

'I'm not!' she insisted, indignantly. 'And I saw them on the beach.'

'*Your* beach?' jeered Hughie, laughing, as he remembered her claim that day he had been sent to find her, 'Whale prints on the sand no doubt.'

Kirsten felt tears of frustration spring into her eyes and turned from the group of laughing men. As she retreated, irritated and hurt, she just caught sight of Sandy, motionless and thoughtful, standing a little apart from the rest. He at least did not ridicule her even though she could see that he did not believe her. She would find that footprint on the hill again. She knew well that in the boggy soil a mark might lie unchanged for months. She would show them.

However, although she scoured the sides of *Meall Sanna* in every free moment in the following week she could find no trace of the strange marks.

July blew in that year with the full force of a north-westerly gale that lasted for five full days. The crofters huddled in their houses unable to do more than keep the peat fires burning and pray that the weather would break. When finally the wind died down and they crept out to inspect the runrigs and search for the beasts, a strange feeling of apprehension settled over the scattered communities of the peninsula. There were reports from several of the crofting hamlets that certain of the animals could not be found – presumably driven over the cliffs by the weather. This was a calamity hard for many to bear.

Then the news filtered through that ten sheep were unaccounted for at the Estate lands at *Camas na Geall* and a sense of communal disaster was felt by all. Everyone that is except for Nana who seemed curiously elated by the news of the Estate's loss. MacPhail was finally convinced that the Estate had not been responsible for the loss of his beasts but thought some strange madness must have possessed them all and driven them into the sea. Only Kirsten wondered, and thought of some wild beast roaming freely during the storm and devouring the wretched creatures. She knew that no one, not even Sandy, would believe her if she told them what she believed and kept quiet.

Chapter 3

The Kerala Brooch

Kirsten could not get the footprints and the missing beasts out of her mind in the succeeding few weeks. She was sure there must be some connection between the two, some great, wild beast roaming free on the hills, a wolf, or a bear, but after the ridiculing she had received from the men, she kept her thoughts to herself. Her grandmother's outburst about McColl also bothered her. Why was she so upset? Who was he anyway? But she knew no one would talk to her about it and brooded quietly over it all. She felt alone and irritated and grew troublesome.

So it was that Sandy found himself one evening, sitting on a rock, fishing and wishing that Jessie had not asked him to perform this 'little duty'.

'You are the only one she listens to, you know,' she had said. 'I never knew such a selfish girl, always off wandering and forgetting to be part of the family. Dreaming, playing and sulking. It's always the same, Sandy. Whenever I have to ask her to do any jobs around the place, she's missing. You are the only one that has any chance of sorting her out for she adores the sight of you.'

And so he let out a deep sigh, shouldered his bag of small cod and coalies and set off in search of Kirsten. Presently he found her, sitting alone on the beach, gazing at the sky and making shapes out of the clouds. Sandy took a place on the sand beside her.

'See that cloud like a great bear?' she said distractedly and pointed above her head.

28

'Ah yes I see it, but what about that salmon over the Sgurr of Eigg?'

'That,' replied the girl simply, 'is a dog.'

Sandy let out a deep sigh. Kirsten was in a sulk. How was he to begin? He'd rather be in a storm in the mid Atlantic than sort the girl out.

'Oh there is no place like Ardnamurchan,' he said after a time, 'wild one minute and so beautifully calm and quiet the next. I can't tell you how much I've missed it all. And you, Kirsten, you're growing into a fine lass. You change every time I am away. I can hardly keep up with you.' And then he added with cunning, 'You will be good at all the things in the croft by now.'

'Oh there are so many things, Uncle Sandy,' she sighed, 'and Mother is always after me to do things for her. She is always going on about something. I don't mind much of the time but whenever I want to be by myself – and come away down here – she demands that I *do* something else. Sometimes I think she just *wants* to make life hard for me. Then, whenever Hughie wants to go and see to his precious ram, no one bothers. It isn't fair. I always have to stay at home and he goes off whenever he likes.'

'Kirsten,' he said, 'have you ever wondered why she wants *you*?' The girl looked sullenly at her feet and did not reply. 'You know that there's so much to do and maybe she really needs you. You know she does not always keep well. What do you think?'

Kirsten half turned her back on him, and pretended not to hear. She was in a sulk and did not want to interrupt her cloud gazing. Sandy studied the girl for a moment and then gazed way out over the sea to where the tops of the Uists were just visible, poking up over the horizon. The air was dry making the islands seem smaller and more distant than usual. After some minutes he spoke.

29

'Do you know what they think about us in India?' he began. 'They think we must be very strange to eat cows. They can't understand that at all.'

She looked at him curiously. For a moment he said no more and waited until he was sure her interest was kindled. Then he reached deep into his pocket, drew out a small package and rested it carelessly in his hand. It was a small scrunch of brown paper, fixed loosely into a parcel with a piece of yellowed wax tape. He made no comment, but watched surreptitiously out the corner of his eye as Kirsten squinted at it with interest. It lay there mysterious and intriguing while Kirsten wrestled between her desire to brood, and her desire to discover the secret of the little packet.

Finally her curiosity got the better of her and she caved in. Looking at him, her head cocked to one side, she waited for him to continue. Sandy made a pretence of coming out of a dwam. 'Oh..., oh..., yes..., see here, Kirsten, I have been meaning to give you this,' and he handed the little paper parcel to the girl.

She pulled the wrapping off eagerly and stared for a moment in wonder. In her hand lay a small brass brooch, curved like a crescent moon and with a blue stone set in its heart.

'What is it, Uncle Sandy? Oh it's really beautiful.'

'Och it's a wee thing I picked up in a market in Kerala, years ago. Only, I thought you might like it now.'

'Kerala?'

'Aye, it's just at the very bottom of India, you see – very hot and teeming with thousands and thousands of people. You should see it! Elephants lumbering along the roads and the palm trees and all fine silks and lace. You would not believe what it's like. Food so hot in your mouth that you think your tongue will burn off and heat in the air that makes you think the whole earth is on fire.'

'It must be very strange indeed!'

Sandy laughed, and looked intently at the girl. 'Not to them! It's all so normal to them. But they would find it hard to understand what you are like! They worship cows, you know, in India.' Kirsten looked puzzled. 'Yes they worship them, but we eat them. They could never understand that.'

Sandy looked out over the sea again as if in a daydream, then he turned back to Kirsten and continued. 'You know I always wanted to go to Kerala and see what it was like, all the time I sat over there in the schoolhouse and dreamed of going to sea. But when I got there all I did was curse the heat and wish I could sit here on this wee bit spit of sand and look at the islands, and hear the gulls crawing in the sky. I was as sick for home as I'd ever been and somehow when I saw this brooch it reminded me of the sea in your little bay, a little splash of blue in the centre of a crescent of shining, golden sand. I've kept it with me these last twenty years, in my pocket, but I think you ought to have it now. Someday you may want to remember this wee spot.'

Kirsten beamed and turned the brooch over in her hand. She could see what Sandy meant – a golden beach by a blue sea.

'It's such a different world there, Kirsten. I could tell you things about Kerala, or for that matter Africa, or the far islands of the Pacific, that you would find impossible even to picture, let alone believe. Why, we were driven, by a gale, onto an island in Papua New Guinea where there are still cannibals and I had a job to face up to the chief and save one of my men. They were fierce and angry because he killed one of their goats and I had to give him nearly a whole herd of the cows we were carrying to Australia to calm him down. Can you imagine what it would be like to live there? Or what about the wee boy that sold me this brooch, in the rat ridden market, with all his worries about heat and flies and feeding his

31

poor sick parents? Can you think what it would be like to be him?'

Kirsten wondered what Sandy was driving at. He was right, she could not imagine anything but her own place.

'And if I'd tried to tell him,' he continued, 'about gathering in the peat or how clear and blue the sky could be on a day when white snow covered *Meall Sanna,* he would have looked at me as if I was a madman. Snow! – he'd never have seen snow in all his life. Or what it would be like to traipse over that hill to the school, all the things you do and take for granted. You know, Kirsten, sometimes it's very hard to get in someone else's shoes and see things the way they do – sometimes especially our friends or our family.' He looked for a light of understanding in Kirsten's face and wondered if she understood him.

'Ye-es,' she said after a lull. But she was remembering how cruelly Hughie and the men had jeered at her, rather than how badly she had been treating her mother. 'People often misunderstand me.'

He shook his head in despair. 'And you, them?'

She grunted noncommittally. Suddenly, Kirsten turned and faced him. 'Uncle Sandy, *you* did believe about the footprint I found, didn't you? You don't think I'm lying do you?'

He was taken aback. Was this what was bothering her? He hesitated; he had not believed her tale about the footprints. 'I don't rightly know, Kirsten. I believe that you saw something. Whether it was a footprint or not, you only can know. What was it like?'

She described it to him. He only looked at her unsurely and finally gave his judgement. 'I'd say it was probably just a churned up spot where a cow walked over its own tracks.'

Kirsten choked back her despair. Why could he not take her word for it? Why were they all so sceptical? They were all as bad at understanding her as she would be at understanding what it would be like to be a market boy in Kerala. Tears of frustration appeared in her eyes. She wanted to tell him about the noises on the beach, explain the footprints there, and how she had seen them. But she could hardly do that, for even yet, she had not owned up to her trip that night, looking for the spyglass. That would only cause more trouble.

'Uncle Sandy...' she began again, suddenly changing the subject.

'Aye?'

'...who's McColl?'

Sandy started and faced her. 'Well people don't like talking about McColl...' he said sharply, stalling.

'But why?'

He waited for a moment before he answered, then making a decision he began to explain. 'The tale goes back to the time of your mother's mother's mother, when all the family lived over at Tornamona on *Ben Hiant*.'

'Where the Estate is now?' she interrupted. 'I never knew they lived over there.'

'Well they don't like to talk about it. The land was very, very good, and the MacPhails, and our folk and some McKinnons and some others all lived there. It was fertile, good ground, and the crofts did well. They had all lived there for generations and generations – since way before *Callum Chille* himself.

'Then one year the Laird decided, without any warning to anyone, mind, to turn the land over to sheep at a single stroke. Twenty-six families turned out on their heels, all for the stupid, woolly beasts. It was a terrible disgrace and a terrible, terrible time. Your grand-mother's father died of the shock, he took the news so bad, and her own sister – a Kirsten like yourself – went off shortly afterwards to America with her husband. She has never seen her since. Some folks followed too, to

America and Canada, and the rest were left to scrape some kind of living from the ground that was left. It was a terrible thing for them to be thrown off *their* land, don't you think?' Kirsten nodded in agreement. 'Imagine being taken from the very land where you lived happily and left to go in search of some other place, not so good or so easy as where you had been.'

For a moment there was a wild look about Sandy and then he continued, 'So your folks came here to this wee bit channel of land that just about gives enough nourishment to the croft and to raise a few sheep. Oh it's nowhere near as good as Tornamona, even if it is so beautiful on a day like this.' He looked around and drew in a deep breath as if tasting the air. 'And that was not all, for one of the Laird's men still went about calling on the rents and making things so, so hard for those that were left on the Estate lands that he was despised. He was McColl the tacksman and more than one called a curse upon him. They say even yet the nettles grow on his grave in the kirk yard in Kilchoan.'

Kirsten looked at her uncle half in disbelief and half in shock at this tale. 'But that's just terrible!' she said indignantly. 'What right had the Laird to throw the people off the land for the sheep?'

'Oh just about every right you can think of. The land was his, and the sheep were his, and the people were having to pay him a rent – oh, he could do just as he pleased – and he did.'

'And this McColl, what kind of man was he?'

'I never heard what he looked like, but I never heard that he was much liked – and can you blame them, hounding the people as he did?'

A new light of understanding entered Kirsten's eyes. 'So that is why Nana's so bitter against the sheep.'

'And the McColls,' continued Sandy, 'though don't you go and be talking about this with her, or anyone else

34

for that matter. Best to keep what you've heard to yourself. Right?'

'Mmmm,' she replied, nodding.

Sandy rose to go. The last deep tints of red were fading over the ocean out west, and the cormorants and gulls were quietening for the night. Over the moor a peewit could be heard calling but other than that there was no sound to be heard. 'You know,' he said, 'I really don't think there is anywhere quite as peaceful as your wee bay, Kirsten, from the Cape to the Pole. Nothing ever happens here at all.'

The girl took the small brooch and looked at it intently for a moment. Yes she could see why it had reminded Sandy of this spot. Carefully she fastened it into the neck of her shawl. She did not realise then, just how much she would think on this small gift in the coming weeks.

'Thank you, Uncle Sandy,' she said and the two walked in the gloaming back towards the village.

Chapter 4

The Loss at Glendrian

Afterwards, whenever she thought about it, Kirsten could not quite remember how she managed to become separated from the rest of the group. The other details of that night were forever etched on her memory. But of the earlier part, only wisps of recollection hung with her.

An urgent thudding came at the door of the croft, and Malcolm McKinnon's voice came bursting in, waking the family.

'Jamie, Hughie, come, come quick!'

'Whatever's the problem?' came the disgruntled reply from within the house.

'The bull's gone missing, and I'm really fearful for it. Will you come? Will you come?'

There was an urgency in his voice and so Jamie and Hughie heaved themselves out from their warm beds, and reluctantly got themselves ready to go out. Jamie was after Malcolm in only a few moments, for he had already set off to rouse the other men of the hamlet.

It was as he stepped through the door, that Hughie had fallen and cried out in pain from the ground, his ankle twisted awkwardly under him. Torn between concern for her son and her husband, Jessie had despatched Kirsten with the lantern in pursuit of the small party, for she reckoned that they would need light that night. She was right.

'Hurry straight back, Kirsten, I'm afraid for you both,'

she had said as she bundled her daughter out of the door.

Kirsten did not catch up with the sortie of men until they were nearly a hundred yards beyond her beach as they worked their way along the rocky headlands towards Carraig Cliffs and Glendrian.

It was windy and a steady breeze was blowing from the north-west whipping up the sea into a froth of white horses, that were just visible to them in the darkness. Kirsten could taste the salt on her lips and the heavy, musty, smell of kelp weed blowing up from the shore. The noise of the waves carried to them loudly as the sea broke upon the rocks then spilled back into the rising, rolling water of the next wave. The men were deep in debate about the course they should take.

'It will probably just have wandered down to Sanna,' Jamie was pleading.

'No! No!' exclaimed the distraught crofter. 'I heard him bellow way over here and he sounded terrified. I am sure we must press on to find the beast, it may trapped on the shore.'

'The wind could have carried the noise, though, Malcolm', suggested another. Like Jamie he had joined this errand grudgingly. It was the middle of the night and he would much rather have been asleep in his bed.

'It's just not like him to be wandering, at all.'

Reluctantly the party agreed to stick with Malcolm's hunch and continue their search.

Jamie turned to his daughter, taking the lantern from her. 'Kirsten, go home,' he said.

Kirsten hesitated. She loved being out at night. The night air and the scent of the chase thrilled her. 'No I'm scared, Father, and besides, Mother *said* I was to stay with you,' she lied. Her mother *might* have meant that she was to come back with him, she reasoned, but in her heart she knew the truth was that she would have expected her to return at once. But Kirsten persuaded herself that she could argue this was what she had understood her mother to mean. It was only a small lie, after all and small lies did not really count, did they? It was, however, the last time Kirsten ever told a lie in all her life.

Jamie regarded her in the dim light of the lantern and gave in. 'Stay close by me then,' he said.

The group passed on to a point where the rocks gave way to a short meadow, cut by a burn where iris and primula were still flowering on its banks. Kirsten knew this spot, for it marked the edge of her usual, solitary wanderings. From here the terrain was more difficult as the rocks broke into a series of crevices and small coves before hitting the shingle beach at the foot of the Carraig Cliff and the caves of Glendrian. It was not easy ground to cover and she tried to follow closely the course her father trod, in the poor light.

It was then that they heard the noise. Across the scraggy rock land came a long, loud, mournful, bellow that chilled every one of their hearts. The whimpering, quivering, howling sound hung on the wind for a moment until it faded off in a final wail. At first, it did resemble the bellow of a bull or a cow, but as it grew it was as unlike the natural call of that beast as could be imagined. What it was that caused it they could not tell, but terror was behind it. The noise was repeated twice more until it was muffled and ceased.

No one moved for several minutes, all listened intently for any other noise. There was none, and Malcolm insisted in pressing on. He calculated that the sound had come from their inland flank and set off at a pace with the others in pursuit. Kirsten trudged on doggedly at the rear, falling a little behind as she struggled to keep up.

She could just make out their dim shapes passing rapidly over the ground a hundred yards ahead and followed as the shadowy forms veered to the left, towards

Carraig Cliff again. Presently the group appeared to halt in the lee of a large boulder that sat in the neck of a small gully. In the shadows, it was not possible to make them out clearly, but Kirsten was glad that they were waiting for her to catch up. She did not want to lose her way. Stumblingly, she drew nearer, panting. Then suddenly she stopped dead in her tracks. In the shadow of the boulder it was not the group of familiar, homely crofters that she saw, but a group of wild looking men, savage and unreal.

In that first instant she took in their wild forms and froze, rooted to the spot by confusion and fear. There were nine or ten of them, each with long hair that fell from the shoulders down their backs. Their arms and chests were bare. Between them, trussed by its legs and hanging on a pole they carried, was a bull – McKinnon's bull. Its eyes bulged with fright. This much Kirsten was able to take in on that first awful glance, but no more for, without any warning, her legs were seized fiercely in a grip from behind that sent her crashing to the ground. In the next moment her arms were drawn behind her and bound with some kind of rope. It all happened so quickly, that she was aware of little more than the fierce tugging at her limbs, the pain at her wrists and the smell of the bog in her nostrils. A rough hand pulled her to her feet and a hand covered her mouth. She tried to wriggle free and scream, but she was held firm.

Kirsten could make no sense of all this. It was as if in the blink of an eye she had been catapulted into an awful dream. She was so scared that she could not think what she ought to do.

A gag was brutishly twisted into her mouth. It tasted dirty and salty and made her feel sick. Now a rough hand pushed her to follow the wild figures who crept on once the moon fell again behind a cloud, swinging the beast on the pole as they went. Kirsten felt the fierce prodding in the small of her back and stumbled on blindly hoping she could make sense of it all and might find some means of escape.

Where oh where were the others? She must have lost sight of them in the darkness. Who were these people? Where were they taking her? Her hands ached where their rough bindings held them and her legs, too were tiring. More than once she fell to the ground sobbing, only to be prodded once more to her feet and forced to go on. If only she had gone home as her father had bidden her.

She could just make out that they were approaching the Carraig Cliff and therefore the great cave of Glendrian. She must try and keep her wits about her. This spot she knew, though she had only once been here before; with her father when they had been setting a creel off the headland and had landed at the foot of the cliff to look for a log to use as a marker. Then she had stood in wonder at the great cleft, a hundred feet high cutting into the rock face at an angle. This was the beginning of the great cave, but Jamie had told her that it only ran back for several hundred feet before ending in a small circular cavern. She had been too scared of the deep darkness within the cave to investigate, and contented herself with exploring the group of shallow cups that formed the other caves of Glendrian. It had seemed so pleasant in the sun of a hot summer's day. It did not seem at all pleasant now.

Now she was being forced into the slit of the great cave and the blackness that met her eyes was so dense and complete that it was impossible to make out anything at all. It was darker than the blackest night. In the next moment she found herself thrown over the shoulder of one of the men who began climbing the wall of the cave. The air around her was cold and smelt musty, of rotting seaweed. They could not be too far inside the cave, for the noise of the sea beating on the rocks was quite clear. Kirsten wanted to cry, but found her eyes strangely dry. Where was her father, Malcolm McKinnon and the rest? Where was she now? Would she ever see her home again?

At last, at some great height within the cave, she was set down upon a ledge of rock. Suddenly the bull gave out the terrified cry she had heard earlier, though in the confines of the rocky space it reverberated and echoed on and on. The poor beast must also be being hoisted up to the ledge. Exploring with her feet she found that it was a narrow ledge with a sheer face on one side and empty space on the other. She could not escape from here. No one, not one single, solitary soul knew where she was. She would be lost to them as mysteriously as the sheep, the cows and now McKinnon's bull. Her tears came now in quiet sobs and Kirsten cursed her stupidity in insisting that she stayed with the men that night. If only she had gone home and not lied to her father.

Chapter 5

The Deep Recesses

It was several hours later, and a calm, serene dawn was beginning to cast its rosy glow over the heather, turning the hill tops orangey-red and reflecting pink off the pools of mist that hung in the shallow hollows of the boglands. Only now did the men discover the full measure of their loss. Jamie had assumed throughout, that Kirsten was behind Old MacPhail who had been lagging a distance to the rear through all the crazy and fruitless chase of that night. Having separated at some point in the darkness, they now gathered at the thrapple of the small pass that led from the shore at Glendrian towards the hamlet of the same name. None could clearly recall when, or where, they had last seen the girl and now it was Jamie who cursed himself for having allowed her to follow.

They returned first to their homes in hope that she had found her way back there, but found no trace of her. And so for the long, hot hours of that day they scoured the countryside for the girl – but in vain. Jessie was distraught and a great worry filled the rest. For as time passed they feared the worst, that she had fallen into some soft and fatal part of the bog and been sucked in, or had fallen over the cliff in the darkness. And so they searched – all the people of Plocaig and Sanna – hope fading as the light of another day faded also into the deep ocean once more.

Kirsten had just regained her breath when silently she

was pulled again to her feet and forced to march on. The path she was on was now descending very gently, and as they walked she tried to take in every small detail round about her. There was a faint dim light ahead and the ground under her feet was of roughened rock. There was no means of knowing how far they were walking but perhaps they had covered no more than half a mile before they halted, once more.

No noise had come from the men, who kept single file ahead of her, driving McKinnon's bull which they had untied, in front of them. The beast let out an occasional low moan which echoed eerily in the confined space. One man followed behind her, making sure that she followed on, prodding her in the back and grunting from time to time. Their figures were no more than darker shadows in the blackness of the tunnel.

They descended through a narrow gap just about Kirsten's height and little wider than two men abreast, before plunging down a steep set of rough steps chiselled out of the rock. The bull stumbled, but somehow managed the path. Down, down they went for some minutes and as they went Kirsten became aware of a growing light around them so that gradually she was able to make out more of her surroundings – and her captors.

What she saw made her despair greater than ever. Wild and fearsome, they looked, half clad, wearing a loincloth of rough skin and in a belt around his waist, each carried either a short handled mallet, or cudgel. Their hair straggled long over their shoulders and upon their chests and backs were intricate tattoos in a winding, serpentine pattern. Under their chins their beards were plaited into a tight knot making their faces look larger and fiercer than ever. They half ran with a low stooping gait keeping their silence all the time. On their legs each wore strange boots – over-large, bulging boots fastened with thongs as far as their knees. They were not long-footed as is a normal shoe, but were practically round and somehow made no sound as they padded on the rocky floor.

Ahead, Kirsten had the impression that the narrow tunnel opened out into a larger space and it was from there that the pale bluish light, which had been growing around them all the while, thrust itself into the passage. It caused large dancing shadows to fall from her captors upon the walls of the tunnel, increasing their eerie menace. The air was warm and humid, unlike the icy coldness of the cave, or the freshness of the air outside where the wind blew across the sea. Kirsten was disorientated and confused.

Suddenly, a rough shove on her shoulder thrust her through a narrow gap and into a small room-like recess off to one side of the tunnel and, before she could resist, a barricade was hurriedly put over the entrance cutting out much of the blue glow. She was alone, completely and utterly alone.

Gradually her eyes strengthened in the dim light and she took stock of her surroundings. The area was no more than a few feet wide, slightly broader than she was tall. She tried the barrier, but it was solidly wedged against the rock and would not budge. There was no furnishing of any kind in the space. Rough rock made the floor, the walls and the ceiling. At the back there was a shallow shelf in the rock where she sat down, rested and considered her situation. Here she was, a captive, deep underground.

No one knew where she was. No one even suspected that this place existed. Did they even know she was missing? The men would still be chasing the bull over the bogs. She was cut off from everything and everyone that she knew. Kirsten hung her head on her chest as hopelessness flowed over her, like a sea closing over the head of a drowning man. She was lost. Kirsten sat, forlorn and afraid – for how long she did not know – until eventually through sheer exhaustion a troubled sleep overcame her.

The loss of McKinnon's bull was a great personal disaster for the crofter, for the beast was very valuable and essential for the good of all the crofters who effectively shared a small herd of cows between them. He did not begin to know how it could be replaced. But no one gave much thought to this for all were consumed with worry and fear for Kirsten.

The women sat with Jessie and offered comfort. The poor woman was so distracted that she could do nothing but sit and rock tearfully in her chair, cursing herself for allowing the girl out at night, at all. Hughie was useless, for his sprained ankle throbbed so painfully that he could do no more than sit in the house and wait with his mother. For all his anger with his sister he too was forlorn, and frustrated, for he wanted to be with the men folk as they organised their search.

All the while, Jamie and the men continued to scour the countryside, and the coast, always hoping for a sight or sound of the girl, but as they searched, their despair grew. There was no sign.

They began at Sanna and worked their way in parties along the coast to the Carraig Cliffs themselves, continuing their sweep across the moors and bogs to Glendrian Village and Achnaha. Some even traversed *Meall Sanna* to Achoshnish and the far flung hamlets on the other side. They walked for miles, in groups spread out all across the countryside and in this way they covered and re-covered the ground of the peninsula.

Sandy and Jamie were never in their beds in those days but stayed out relentlessly searching, looking, hoping.

But no matter how hard they looked there was nothing, not a sign, not a trace, not a piece of clothing nor a footprint. It was as if the girl had evaporated into thin air.

When she awoke Kirsten was confused at first by the hard floor and the darkness. Then the awful truth came back to her as she remembered the night before. She was a prisoner not knowing even where she was or (more importantly) how she was going to escape, for escape she must.

Very carefully she sat up, straining her ears for any sound that might give a hint of what was likely to happen next. The sound of water dripping onto a hard surface echoed around her and drifting faintly through the half darkness she thought she could just make out the sound of voices. Her heart leapt and a ridiculous hope filled her. She was found! Her father and the others must have found some trace of her and had come to her rescue.

But no sooner had this thought come than it was dashed. For these were low, growling, guttural voices, unlike the soft, lilting tones of the crofters, she knew so well. They were unfamiliar and threatening. Though she strained hard to hear what they were saying the sounds were too faint to make out clearly and the snatched words sounded of an alien and strange tongue. Her hopes thus dashed, she threw herself down on the floor once more in despair.

There was nothing she could do but wait. Kirsten's hand strayed to the brooch that fixed the neck of her shawl and closed tightly around it. The Kerala brooch! The blue stone and the curve of the brass pressed into the palm of her hand and, though she could not see the brooch in the dim light of the cave, suddenly she could see, in her mind's eye, her beach; the curve of the sand

and the sea lapping on the shore. She thought of Sandy and her family and home and somehow the brooch brought her closer to them. This gave her courage. Sandy had faced all kinds of danger and had never given up hope. She must not either.

It seemed a long, long time before a noise roused her as the barricade was loosened and a platter with some food was thrust roughly through the opening.

It was difficult to make out exactly what was being provided. It smelt salty and musty. Kirsten, ravenously hungry, fell upon it, unappetising as it was. At least they did not appear to mean her any immediate harm if they were taking the trouble to feed her. It was a vegetable of sorts, something she did not recognise, strong and salty and quite chewy.

Once the plate was empty she picked it up and licked it clean. It was then that a curious thought struck her. The platter was made of heavy stone yet was perfectly round. Even in that dim light she was able to make out that it was ornately decorated with a running pattern on its outer edge and had glass like stones set in it at regular intervals. This was unlike the simple china and wooden bowls they used at home. It was heavy and ornate. Where had it come from?

Presently she was aware once more of voices, deep and throaty, echoing in the cavern outside her cell. They were nearer now and easier to hear. Foreigners of some kind! But where did they come from and why did they live here, hiding away in holes and caves in the ground? Who were they? Pirates hiding with their loot and treasure? Or wild men from the north? A memory came of Sandy sitting in the crofthouse telling his tales of peoples across the world. He had said that there were still pirates in the South China Sea, and even off Africa. But why would they come here?

Quite suddenly a realisation struck her, like a horse

kicking you in the stomach, and she caught her breath in amazement. These men, whoever they were, were speaking a strange tongue, and yet somehow, Kirsten was able to make out what they were saying. It sounded familiar and unfamiliar all at the same time and it took her a while to grasp why. Many of the words she recognised, for they sounded quite like something she knew, but they were often in the wrong order or seemed to be pronounced in a strange way. Yes, the language was very like her own Gaelic – a rough half grown Gaelic, with odd throaty gurgles and rasping, choking noises where she would have sighed or lilted in her mouth. It was a strange tongue and yet she could quite easily understand it. How could this be? Who were these people who spoke a little like her? She had to know. Perhaps she could even persuade them to let her go.

Kirsten cleared her throat and called out in a dry, cracked voice, 'Please! Please help me, I want to go home.'

Silence fell, like a door shutting out a howling wind. The voices ceased and no sound could be heard save the slow, monotonous dripping of the water on the rock.

Chapter 6

The Cavern of the Lochan

For an age Kirsten lay in the blackness, wishing that she had not drawn attention to herself. The silence was worse than the speech, for somehow the sound of human voices, however strange, was comforting. This was like being entombed, being buried alive. Was she going to be left here for ever?

Eventually, without any warning, the barricade was loosened, swung to the side and a low squat man, dressed as the others had been, in a rough loincloth and the peculiar, round boots, motioned to her with a jerk of his head to follow. Kirsten did not dare speak now, but obediently followed in the steps of the man, as he shambled off with a stooping, lolling gait in the general direction of the light.

The path soon widened out into an open space around thirty yards across. Kirsten became aware of a number of openings and recesses in the walls of what was apparently a long thin, cavern. Here and there she thought she could see a pair of eyes peering at her cautiously and curiously from these shadows, darting from her vision if she chanced to meet them. They flickered and glowed and then drew off. The man shuffled on, taking no notice of this, but turned round occasionally to check that she continued to follow. He seemed content. No word was spoken, Kirsten followed on meekly.

This passage in turn widened into a larger cavern, the roof of which was so high she was unable to make it out.

At the end of this was an opening through which a brighter blue light broke into the gloom. They continued towards it. The final opening was narrow. Kirsten managed it with ease, but a large man would have had to wriggle to pass through it, and here she received the greatest shock and wonder of all. For several moments she stood absolutely still gaping at the sight.

The area that they had passed into was an immense cavern. There was enough light to see reasonably clearly, like an evening light. She was standing on a highish rise at one edge of this vast space so that her view stretched as far as the other side of the great cave, several miles off! From her feet a series of rocky outcrops and skerries, fell down to the shore of a large expanse of water, bigger than any loch she had ever seen, for the lochans of Ardnamurchan are small, peaty and dark. The lochan was perhaps two miles wide and several miles long, and within it was set a number of small, rocky islands.

Gradually Kirsten took in that it was the water itself that gave the unearthly light. The lochan glowed with a blue luminescence that rose from it and spread into the space of the cavern, reflecting off the rock, which glistened and sparkled as if a film of diamonds covered its surface. It was breathtakingly beautiful and for a short while Kirsten forgot her fear and stood entranced with the wonder of it. It was as if all the stars of the heavens had been captured and embedded on the walls and the ceiling of this cave, glistening and twinkling, and that the sky had been caught and rolled out as a carpet on the floor. The air was warm and balmy like the breeze on a summer evening. Here was a whole world, fantastic and bizarre, beautiful and entrancing, somewhere under the familiar, heavy bogs and rocks of her home. An alien land juxtaposed to her world, so different and yet so brilliant in its own way.

A snort brought her back abruptly from her thoughts. Her guide now pointed to a path that led from the escarpment where they stood and along the shore of the luminous loch. The two set off, making their way quite easily across the rocks, for the way was well marked and a run of smooth steps told of the passage of many, many years of feet wearing them down, polishing them like glass. It ran on through a gap and under a rocky overhang, until presently Kirsten was aware that the ground under her was no longer hard, barren rock, but soft and springy like grass. Closer inspection revealed a hairy, frondy moss-like plant spreading like a meadow over the ground, and here and there, small purple, orchids and orange daisies formed clusters like a patchwork on its surface. The ground rose gradually into a small hillock and this hid from view the part of the cavern where the loch stopped and the meadow appeared to fall off into the distance. It was an easy, gentle climb and all the time Kirsten was aware of the pleasantness of the air. It was fresh and warm and yet very still.

As they gained the summit Kirsten again halted involuntarily in wonder at what she saw. Nestling in a small valley a hundred feet below her was a group of structures of rough stone, round and clustered together adjacent to a series of cave like openings in the walls of the rocks. From one of these issued a torrent of water in a white, frothy fall and this swirled and eddied into a large pool from where a stream gently meandered across the meadow until it was hidden from view.

To her amazement in a corralled area to one side were a small flock of less than a dozen sheep and a few cows – and if her keen eyesight were not mistaken, McKinnon's bull. Kirsten stood, amazed. This was no pirate kingdom, yet what it was, her confused mind could not yet work out. Again she was summoned by a grunt from her guide, already several paces away from her and waiting impatiently for her to continue.

Unquestioningly she pursued his shambling form towards this settlement – it had to be a settlement, and as she did so her curiosity was rising. Who were these people?

'Crallogh, yow brung gurrl?' A taller, more muscular version of her guide addressed the squat man.

'Yus, Choan,' he answered, nodding and pointing to the spot outside the wall of the dwelling where he had grunted and indicated to Kirsten to wait.

'Didd the gurrl struggle when yow brung her hither?'

'Na!' He shook his head slowly 'She dud cumm easily hither.'

'That is gude at least, Crallogh. But yow have nagt dunn well. Yow should nagt have brought her tow the cave. Why dudd yow brung her from the outside any ways?'

'What ellse could be dunn, Choan?' He spoke angrily and glowered at the taller man. The gurrl saw uss, she would have spoken, whott else could be dunn?'

Choan looked at him unhappily. 'This is badd, Crallogh. We musst be thunking what is to be dunn with her.'

'Graccch!' the other snorted, 'Yow should know, should not yow! Yow arre the head ufter all.'

The other ignored this comment but observed anxiously, 'May-haps the Mullach himself will wunt tow thunk what must be dunn. We had best be keepung the gurrl hereby.'

The squat man looked nervous and echoed the words, '*The Mullach*' in a reverential, almost fearful tone.

'Yus, ut is nagt altogether good, Crallogh. Ut is a great pity thut she was brung tow here at all. Brung her tow me, now-times.'

'Yus, Choan.' And with that the squat man stomped

off towards Kirsten and brought her before the taller man, who motioned to her to sit upon a bench of stone carved on its edge with an intricate design. He stared at her, long and intently, uttering no word. But although he looked hard at her, Kirsten did not feel threatened. He was curious, questioning, puzzled. And as he stared, Kirsten stared back deep into his deep, blue eyes, blue as the sea (though the blue sky-like light that filled this strange world, cast a bluer tinge upon everything). It seemed to her that they were as ancient as the world itself. He looked as if had been carved from the very stone of the ground. His face was angular, chiselled and granite grey in colour. His hair too, was grey and swept back from his face into a long mane that hung half way down his back. The hands were those of one used to working with them, callused, gnarled and bent around the fingers, but he stood tall, erect and proud unlike the shambling form of the stooped, old Crallogh.

What he saw in her, Kirsten could not tell, but the eyes seemed to penetrate deep into her and she had to look away. She did not know how to speak and being fearful of being shut off again, waited. Might she yet wake up and find that this was all a crazy dream? A noise to her rear distracted her attention once more, and turning she saw a small group of curious faces peering out from one of the crevices in the rocks. Choan motioned to them to join him and there formed round the girl a semicircle of around fifteen people – mostly men, two or three women and several scraggy children. They too sat and stared at her, unblinking and silent.

Finally Kirsten was unable to bear it any longer and broke the silence.

'Please,' she said quietly, 'I just want to go home.' There was a sudden sharp intake of breath from her audience, as if they could not believe their ears. No one moved. No one spoke. 'Please,' she said again, ' I only want to see my family and go home. Please do not keep me here.' The silence was held, as a breath is held before a blow. Kirsten felt uneasy under their steady, enquiring gaze. If only they would respond. 'Please…'

Choan took a long, deep breath and then replied, slowly, a startled tone evident in his rough, deep voice. 'Yow speke like uss?'

'Yes, something like it, I suppose,' answered Kirsten brightening a little. 'I… I… understand you at least. Please, I only want to go home. Do not keep me here, please.'

'Ut us nagt forr me to speke about such thungs. The Mullach musst be deciding what musst be dunn. Ut us nagt forr us. Yow musst be waiting tull yow can be brung tow the Mullach. For now-times yow musst wait with us. We wull be keeping after yow. We mean yow na harm.'

Kirsten understood quite clearly what Choan was saying and evidently he too could understand her. But she also grasped what he was meaning and did not like what she was hearing one bit. 'But why must I stay here?' she cried despairingly. 'I can do you no harm. I am only a child and all I want is to see my family. Surely you can see that,' she sobbed. A note of desperation was creeping into her voice again. Surely they could understand that she was only a girl. They had children of their own right there beside her, hadn't they?

'The Mullach.' was all he replied. 'The Mullach wull decide. Ut us nagt forr us.'

'You brought me here from my home. Why must I stay? Why? Why?' she asked desperately. But no matter how much she persisted Choan bluntly refused to make any further comment, and the rest of the company, following his example remained silent also. It was clear that there was nothing she could do but wait. Wait for this Mullach, probably, whoever, or whatever he was. Yet she was determined to try and find some way of escape if she could, and decided to watch for the faintest opportunity that might come her way. Awareness might give her that chance and she would look for it like a Kestrel watching for a field mouse.

For the present no one spoke another word but all began to go about their business almost ignoring her (although Kirsten was bright enough to realise that one of the men was always nearby, watching her, guarding her, never letting her out of their sight).

She too watched earnestly, for she decided that if she were to escape she must take in every detail about this world which now surrounded her that might help her. It was a surreal world of constant light, steady warmth, and soft quiet noises – nothing seemed to alter or change with the passing hours, unlike the shifts of light and weather and tide that filled her life in Plocaig. Oh how she longed for the sounds and smell of the sea, the wind and the weather. She often gazed at the brooch and thought of home.

A ceaseless glow flowed from the luminescent loch and so it was not possible to tell whether it was day or night or how much time was passing in her own world. The only sign that time moved on was when meals were prepared and eaten and at certain times when the people would gather in the small stone structures and sleep. Here curtains fashioned of a rough, coarse material of plaited strands or skins were drawn over the openings of the shelters, which were otherwise completely solid and impervious to light, so that Kirsten realised that in this rainless, weather-less world they offered shelter only from the light itself, giving the peace of darkness in which to sleep.

In the waking hours she followed the group as they walked to the loch and pulled in fish using nets strung out between small round coracles in which they paddled about on the surface. The nets, when she examined them closely, were woven of a crude cord of seaweed strands and this she recognised as the same material that had bound her hands the night of her capture.

But it was the loch and the fish that were most astounding. The water was absolutely teeming with life. Myriads of minuscule and barely visible shrimps swirled and swarmed in the water, and it was these that gave off the light. Each shone with a faint, pale-blue, fluorescent glow, but in their multitude they caused the water to radiate and shimmer as if the sun were reflecting from its surface. Yet it was clear that the loch was very deep, for in small, faint patches the luminescence was broken where the shoals of shrimps moved off revealing that they occupied only the superficial reaches of the water.

Beneath them the presence of a deep, inky blackness suggested an immense depth. The loch was salty, like the sea, and seals played farther out, small half-matured seals almost like pups. Shoals of fish darted through the shrimps, feeding – fish as she had never seen before, ugly, large eyed fish, bright yellow bellied with massive jaws and three large spikes on their dorsal fins – fish used to hunting in the black, impenetrable depths of the loch. These fish formed the staple diet of the people, along with weed that they harvested from the shore and ate.

The few sheep and cattle were grazed upon the meadow of moss, poor confused beasts that seemed completely out of place in this underworld. The people, however, seemed used to tending livestock as they handled the animals with care and attention. Some were used for food, the cows for milking and their hides for clothing. On one occasion she found another corralled area with large tusked beasts that snorted and grunted noisily. She had seen pictures like these in books. They were wild boars, hairy snouted, with tusks that could skewer a man. But none lived in Scotland anymore –

except here; ancient beasts hidden in the primeval depths of the ground.

There was no wood or fuel of any kind in the cavern and at first Kirsten wondered how they would cook the meal or whether she would have to eat the fish raw. After their first trip to the loch, the group, men women and children, (they seemed to form an extended family) continued past their dwellings and into one of the caves near the waterfall. The water of the fall was fresh, icy and pure and Kirsten had thought at first that it was the spray arising from this, as it hit the rocks that formed a misty cloud around the mouth of the cave. However, she soon discovered that it was not spray, but steam, for as they entered she became aware of heat and saw to her amazement a round cleft in the ground in which water boiled and bubbled, steaming water, heated from the very bowels of the earth itself. The fish and the weed were placed on stone troughs and lowered into this cauldron, where it was boiled through and then shared evenly about.

Everything about their way of life was strange and yet ordered and even homely. Kirsten began to see that they were little different from her, scraping a life from the land, but how she longed to be free.

One thing that had puzzled her was soon solved. On the shore of the lochan grew a great, leathery weed with giant, hollow, round pods. This the men cut and fashioned to form their boots. The soft fleshy belly of the pods was arranged in clumps and Kirsten could see why she had mistaken their imprint for that of an animal and also why their footsteps were so cushioned and silent. These were the ideal shoes for the hunter who wanted to remain silent as he stalked his prey.

The people fished, cooked, ate and slept, conversing only with each other when out of Kirsten's earshot. For the most part she followed and watched and waited. She was not sure by which path she had been brought to the cavern, for there were many openings in the rocks, leading to other caverns or long dark passages. Escape she must, but how?

Once, when she had thought all the occupants of the dwelling were sleeping, she had cautiously attempted to leave and creep out of the door. But as she pulled back the curtain she had seen the form of Crallogh rise from among the slumbering forms, his face staring stonily at her, and she had let go, leaving it to fall gently back into place. She was being watched more closely than she had hoped.

Chapter 7

The Homeless

Three days had passed since Kirsten's disappearance, the small, close-knit community at Sanna and Plocaig were miserable and dejected. Everyone felt the loss deeply. From Kirsten's home came the sound of endless sobbing as her mother, inconsolable, clung to a faint hope that Kirsten would yet be found safe. The weather remained hot and dry, and far into the evening Jamie and Sandy stretched themselves, covering and recovering the ground. Jamie had walked the six miles over the rough track to Kilchoan and the other villages to the south of the peninsula, giving the news of their loss, calling on everyone to keep a lookout for her, always hoping that some sign might have been seen of his daughter.

Now, high on the hills above the caves Sandy stood alone and looked around him. The wind was bending the heather gently and he could see cormorants diving into the waters off the cliffs below him, feeding on mackerel. Over the humped peaks of Rum sparse white clouds rode in an orange sky as the sun bent once more to its rest and off the shore of Muck a masted skiff was visible plying the waters. At any other time he would have been content, but not now. He turned and scanned the country toward *Meall Sanna* where deer could be seen running in the hollow crevasse that passes over the left shoulder of the hill. Everything was as peaceful and tranquil as it should be, the happy scene of his home, but he was utterly miserable in his heart.

He was leaning against an outcrop of tumbled rock

and scree. The land here was scarred with a large cleft and the wind whistled through the rocks. For a moment he thought he heard a low grumbling sound as of a voice calling, and leapt to attention, listening. But now it seemed more like a crowd of voices, rhythmic and chanting. It was a faint sigh of a sound that hung for a moment in the air and then faded with the wind. Again he thought he heard it, groaning, and he hoped against hope that it was Kirsten.

Carefully he hunted the ground where he was standing, but save for a few huge boulders there was nothing that could hide her. The sound came again. Was it a trick of his ears, teasing him because of his hope? He put his head to the cleft in the rock and felt a trace of warm air against his cheek, warmer than the chill wind that evening; this was strange – he could not account for that. Again the sound. It seemed to have a rhythm. He strained hard to hear it and then a seagull crying overhead drowned it out.

Still the wind continued to whistle through the cleft until Sandy finally convinced himself that the noise was no more than a trick of the wind. Turning, he retraced his steps heavily, towards Plocaig.

Deep under the ground in the quiet world of the stone men Kirsten was despairing of finding any means of escape. Four meals and two sleep-times had passed since Choan had last addressed her. All that time she had tagged along with them, watchful, intrigued but always looking for her opportunity. None had come.

The people were in the main kind to her, offering her a share of their food and making sure she was comfortable. Kirsten began to feel less fearful of them, only miserable at her own situation.

She was sitting on a rock outside the cooking cave

looking at the lochan shimmering in the distance and wondering what her family had made of her disappearance. Were they still looking for her or had they given up hope of finding her by now? A hand touched her shoulder and she looked up into the concerned face of one of the women.

'Yow arre unhappie?' she whispered.

'Yes,' replied Kirsten as she looked down at her feet. 'I want to go home to my mother.'

'Shhh! Dow nagt speke so lowd. Choan wude nagt like uss tow be speaking at all.' Kirsten nodded. 'Yess I cann see why yow arre unhappie. Here, have thus fude,' and she handed her a stone platter with some of the boiled fish on it. Kirsten took it and ate hungrily. 'Yowr muther,' continued the woman, 'Uss she oald?'

'No, but she is not always well,' whispered Kirsten back to her. Her companion looked even sadder and shook her head.

'She wull be wurse now yow are nagt there.' Kirsten felt a tug in her throat. The woman continued, 'Ut us nagt so good hereby I amm sure. Wull yow tell me of the high lands. I havve olways wunted tow go tow there, butt oanly the hunturs arre allowed. We musst remain hereby und wait forr them tow returrn. Tell me, is ut grate? Arre therre really tow grate lights un the sky like the oald menn say?'

'Oh yes,' said Kirsten, 'two great lights, the moon by night and the sun, hot and bright in the day.' Tears filled her eyes as she spoke. She felt more far away from her home than ever. The woman seemed to notice.

'Ut us nagt gude that yow arrre nagt wuth yowr people,' said the woman.

'But... you, will you help me get back to my family and my home?' asked Kirsten eagerly.

The woman sighed deeply and opened her mouth again to speak but at that moment, from nowhere, a blow sent Kirsten reeling from her perch and the platter spinning from her hand. 'What on earth?' she cried out as she fell to the ground.

A rough and loud voice cried out,'Yow arre nagt welcumm hereby. Yow arre nagt wunn of uss! Dow nagt speke tow her Aros, yow remember whot Choan said.'

Kirsten looked up trying to regain her wind. Above her stood a boy perhaps a few years older than she was. He had a bitter, spiteful face which was pulled into an angry scowl.

'Go Aros. Go awae!' he shouted. 'Yow musst nagt speak tow the gurrl.' The woman slunk away but as she did so she cast Kirsten a pitying look. The boy glared at Kirsten for a moment, 'I am Urick, the son of Choan,' he said, 'I am watching yow.' And with that he spat on the ground, turned and left. He walked with a limp for around one foot and ankle he wore a clumsy, dark bandage. Judging from its tattered appearance it had been in place for a considerable time. It was grubby and matted with black, dried blood. Kirsten shuddered.

It was a strange little community. Choan was clearly the senior member for he took the lead in all of their activities and they all deferred to him. When he spoke, they did his will, be it fishing, cooking or eating. All that is except Crallogh, who would grunt and shamble off on some business of his own. Kirsten caught him glaring darkly at Choan, when the other was unaware. What his business was or the meaning of his looks she could not tell.

After her brief talk with Aros, the people spoke only with each other and usually out of Kirsten's earshot. She began to feel lonelier than ever and sat cradling the brooch in her hand, thinking of home. Then quite unexpectedly, after a meal Choan turned to her suddenly and said, 'Yow musst be seen near-times when the

Mullach comes frum Tioradh, this nexst meal-time.'

Kirsten's first feeling was relief at being included in conversation once more after all the silence and isolation. But Tioradh? – Tiree? Surely he could not mean that the passages of this underworld stretched as far as Tiree – the island she knew at the edge of her horizon, thirty miles off beyond Coll and Mull? How far did this kingdom reach? 'Tioradh,' she echoed weakly. A feeling of emptiness and of her smallness descended on her once more If this land were that large she was surely lost to her world for ever.

Choan looked at her, confused. 'Ya, Tioradh. But why urr yow sadd? I said that we mean yow na harm. Yow wull be safe here like the Pixts uss safe.'

'What do you mean the Picts?'

'We arre the remnunts of the Pixts. The great race of the high lunds.'

Vaguely Kirsten remembered her schoolmaster, Mr Shearer, talking of an ancient race that had once lived in Scotland, a people 'of the North'. But she thought they had eventually been conquered and subdued by the incoming Celts, or had been lost in the darkness of history. 'The Picts?' she asked again, bewildered.

Choan rested his large frame back against a rock and looked perplexed at her question. He considered the girl intently for a while and then a look of resolution entered his eyes as he began to speak once more, slowly, thoughtfully, carefully, it seemed.

'How arr yow called?' he asked, gently.

'Kirsten,' came her reply. No one had asked her anything about herself to this point and she felt strangely relieved.

'Churstun,' echoed Choan in his deep, growly drawl, 'yow were found in the high lands by Crallogh and yow neverr knew about the blue-lands wherre we arr now-times?'

'No.'

He sighed and stretched his long legs flat against the ground. 'I spose that now-times would be right to tell yow of the Pixts.' She looked at him blankly wondering where this was leading. Choan continued, 'Menny, menny Orbed-times ago...'

'Orbed-times?' she broke in.

Choan ignored her and continued as if he had not heard her, '...five thousand Orbed-times or more, owr people lived un the high lands, over in the lands whare the bugg light rises into the sky from the sea.' He motioned to one side with his big, broad arm. 'But owr race wus driven over the high lands by fighting peoples tull owr peoples setteled in the high lands hereby, where the bugg light falls into the sea.' He swept his arm to the other side. Kirsten understood that they had come from the east to settle in the west, where the sun sets in the ocean. Again she thought of home and the sun setting over the islands.

'Here they lived forr thousands of Orbed-times,' he continued. 'Ut was a fine land und owr people werr happy, living underr the bugg light und the luttle light. They fushed und hud some cows butt nun of the luttle white cows.' Kirsten looked perplexed but following a nod of Choan's head understood. Sheep! Choan continued his story, and some of the children gathered round listening (as they had obviously often listened before) – all, that is, save Urick who scowled suspiciously and set himself down on a rock a short distance off with his back turned. 'We hudd the sea und the islands und the hills und werr verry content, tull wun day down from the way of the cold wunds, came menn in bottes. Fierce, angry, cruel menn and drove our families unto the sea. They drove uss frum the land and culled most of owr people. Ded, ded, menny ded,' he shook his head sadly. 'Only wun famuly survived. A poor, fearful famuly, a man, a wuman, and three chuldren. The remnunt of the true Pixts. All the risst werr losst, culled on the high lands or driven unto the sea.

But the famuly fledd to the great cave to find safety und by chance fell unto the great passage thut brot them to lochan blue. Never hud eny mann seen the great wurld of the blue lochan before-times. Butt this famuly took refuge there und hoaped to be free some-times. They found ut was a good lund und they werr so afraid tow return tow the high land, that forr ever sunce owr people havv lived here, safe. Safe frum enyman. Yow thunk that the high lands arr really yowr people's lands, but they arr owrs und sum day we wull be returrning tow them. Wun day at the Orbed-time we wull know when. Ut us not right that owr lands should havve been taken fromm uss.'

A cold light, the light of a fanatic, leapt for a moment into his eye and a murmuring growl of discontent arose from the rest of the group. Kirsten shuddered. There was a wild look about Choan and for a moment she remembered her grandmother, fierce and embittered at home, blaming McColl for the loss of their homeland. Choan regarded her and misread her thoughts. 'Yow arr right tow be sad, Churstun, it woss wrong to loose owr land.'

She turned her face to him and looked at him through eyes brimming with tears of frustration. 'But, Choan it is a land now where my people live. You cannot go back there. It is my place. I must go back.'

'We wull be going back,' he said. 'Ut is the lund of the Pixts.' He stared at her with steely blue eyes and leapt to his feet, red faced and angry. 'The land uss nott yowrs forr the keeping. Some time the Pixts wull return.'

Kirsten attempted to keep her cool. 'Choan,' she said, 'why will you not let me go home?'

This seemed to irritate him further. 'We arr nott ready yett to returrn to the high lands, we urr still too few. Yowr

65

people might take thus lund fromm us too.'

'But I am not a threat to you and my poor family would not believe me even if I told them that you lived here?'

'No,' he said, 'The Mullach wull decide... and the Orbed.'

'Who is the Mullach?', she asked, ' and what is this Orbed?' But after this she could gain nothing from him for he withdrew once more to silence, leaving Kirsten to ponder his strange story and wonder what it all meant.

It was after the next meal and the family were at their usual fishing point. Another group of stone men were already by the lochan and seemed intent on spoiling the catch of Choan's family. One thrust Choan's coracle out into the lochan where a current carried it far into the distance. Others were cutting through their nets. A wiry scowling man squared up to Choan and Crallogh, a fierce look in his eyes. He shouted angrily at them, waving his arms around excitedly and although Kirsten was unable to understand what passed between them she knew that these were dark threats.

Then abruptly the wiry man lunged at Choan, flailing his stone headed mattock above his head. With a deft twist Choan dodged to the side, but too late – the mattock still struck him a glancing blow on the temple. Blood spurted from an open wound. With a lurch Choan was now on the other man pinning him to the ground. The other kicked him hard but Choan was by far the stronger and held him fast. Blood from his wound blurred his vision, but he shook him violently and raised his own cudgel to strike a blow. Choan held his arm high above the other man's head ready to strike, but then a disgusted look broke through the anger that was set upon his brow and he let it fall weakly by his side, without making a blow. Now he shook the other man again and tossed him to the side, like a sheaf of hay. The wiry individual was badly winded but drew himself to his feet and began to slink off with his fellows, cursing Choan and his family loudly. 'We wull be revenged onn yow, Choan,' he spat out. 'Yow wait. We wull be revenged.'

Choan for his part pulled himself erect and called after him, 'Be gone and bewayrre, Morlech. Do nagt meddul wuth my famuly. We arre great un the race of the Pixts.'

Chapter 8

The Arrival of The Mullach

The first sight that she had as they reached the top of the hillock caused a shiver to creep over her skin. Up until this point her hopes had been relatively high, but now they plummeted and she felt more anxious than ever.

They had walked for about an hour over the meadow and skirted the lochan to reach the farther side of the cavern. All the while they had passed small clusters of stone dwellings such as the one she had already seen, a dozen or more of them. Here and there snatched visions of stooping forms flitting out of the shadows and moving generally in the same direction had begun to make her feel uneasy. But when they reached their vantage point above this dell she saw below her a crowd far larger than she had imagined and she was afraid.

The hollow was roughly circular, a natural amphitheatre of grey rock broken here and there by clumps of green moss. Seated in rows, on rough benches carved out of the rock were groups of men, women and children. There must have been six or seven hundred, at least. All wore the same rough cloth or sealskins as tunics or loincloths. Most were barefooted but some had the large circular boots on their feet. Their skin was slate grey in colour, stiff and waxy, and to Kirsten they seemed more than ever to have been hewn from the rock itself, cold, angular and hard.

In the centre of the space a dais like structure stood on an elevation surrounded by a mound of boulders and rubble, which glistened and glimmered in the glow, casting dancing, sparkling, lights upon the faces of the people, like the sun reflecting off a shimmering pool in a river. Behind the dais, carved into the rock of the walls and roof of the cavern, were the figures of two huge stone men, their hands held aloft, their beards plaited under their chins, in every way the image of the men folk that filled the dell at that very moment.

'Choan...' ventured Kirsten, uneasily. She had been trying to get him to speak to her on the journey, but with no success; he remained withdrawn and morose, strangely anxious, she thought. 'Choan, what will happen?'

'Yew musst nagt speke, yet a-whiles. Cumm, Churstun.' He answered firmly, For a moment he held her gaze with his eyes. They were as blue as the lochan and in them she found the faintest shimmering hint of support and warmth. Yet, in them Kirsten also detected, disquiet. He was sweating slightly at the temples. Choan looked nervous and unhappy.

She followed as she was bidden and joined Choan's family as they took their place near the edge of the assembly, high on the curve of the dell on a long, flat, well worn rock. Kirsten was uncomfortably aware of the stares of many eyes boring into her and looked firmly at the dais to keep her composure.

A sudden swelling chant arose and the people began banging their hands upon their thighs, calling out 'Mullach! Mullach! Mullach!' along with a rhyme or incantation that Kirsten could not make out. The noise echoed and rang off the stone making the din sound like the voices of thousands rather than hundreds. Kirsten cowered behind Choan and held her hands over her ears to block out the noise.

All of a sudden the uproar died off to a quiet, awed whisper like the echoes of rumbling thunder falling off into the distance, as into the dell came the stooped form of a wizened old man. On his head was a dress of shells and round his neck, on a cord, hung a deep green stone, the colour of a jade sea tossed on a wild, windy day. Close behind followed a retinue of several men. The Mullach had arrived. Every eye in the hollowed amphitheatre was fixed upon him as he made his way through the parting crowd. The sight of him sent a pang of fear into Kirsten's throat. She felt further now from her own home and life than ever. All hope fled from her.

Slowly, with purpose, the Mullach ascended steps to the dais, set himself down upon a great flat rock and surveyed the crowd. A complete silence followed. No one moved for several minutes until the Mullach himself slowly rose to his feet once more. Kirsten, half hidden behind Choan's great frame held her breath and dug her fingernails into her palms to stop herself from screaming.

Then the Mullach spoke. His voice had the rasping gurgling tones of the stone men, but for all his physical frailty it was strong and carried easily. 'The Mullach hass cumm for the Great Council, to settle all thatt musst be dun now-times before the Orbed-time cumm. Yowr hearts must be right und pure before the Orbed. Who hass need of the wusdum of the Mullach?'

A man rose from his place and called out bitterly, 'Yow are great und wyse, oh Mullach. My bruther huss wronged me badly. Yow musst decide now-times whot us to be dunn. He huss stoalen of my famuly's food und culled wun of owr animuls.'

Kirsten listened as the man made his complaint to the Mullach. It was long and bitter. Then another rose and gave his side of the story. A battle of words flowed back and forth until at last the Mullach stood. Silence fell and he gave a judgement. Then raising the green stone that hung around his neck high above his head he cried out, 'So thiss us whott I have decidedd. Now-times swear upon the Green Orbed thatt yow will keep this juddgement, for eny promiss madde upon the green stone musst be keppt, utt can never be brokenn, by eny mann.' The two men stood forward and both made an oath upon the green stone and as they returned to their places the Mullach cried out again, 'Reememberrr, yowr promiss is made, und can nagt be brokenn for yow have sworn ut upon the Green Orbed.'

For what seemed like hours a steady barrage of questions, and problems were addressed to the Mullach by individuals rising in their places and calling out in their throaty voices for his opinion and wisdom. Many, it seemed to Kirsten, were to settle grievances and disputes that certain families had with others, and on several occasions she thought that the tension, palpable in the air, would erupt into fighting as men glowered and shouted at each other and waved their clubs above their heads. It was a bitter and unhappy assembly but always the Mullach gave a decision and with no further objection the people would bow to him and accept the outcome.

Kirsten felt increasingly uncomfortable and the words of Choan rang loudly in her memory, *'The Mullach musst decide.'* What would this stooped wizened old man decide for her? What right had he to decide her fate? She did not want to be here. They had no right to keep her here. And yet she knew that her time must come, her future lay in his hands and there was nothing she could do about it. Choan was sweating and Kirsten could sense that he was fearful and uncomfortable at the prospect of addressing the Mullach himself. She pulled herself as far behind Choan's back as she could, trying to keep out of the Mullach's line of view.

A lull fell over the council for a moment and the Mullach cast his gaze slowly over the crowd. Kirsten took in the sweep of his eye as it swung backwards and forwards over the silent upturned faces, taking them in, recognising them, searching them for further problems or dissent. He scanned them slowly seeing deep into their hearts, she thought, an eye searching, probing, seeking, seeing.

And then his eye fell upon her. It stopped dead in its tracks. She saw the pupil widen and flare, the iris quiver, his lids pull back in consternation. It stared and then slowly he raised his hand and pointed straight at Kirsten. With a curl of a long nailed, gnarled finger he silently demanded that she leave her place and approach him. Kirsten looked around in panic.

Choan rose and said to her, 'Cumm and do nagt be afraid. The Mullach wull decide whot is to be dunn wuth yow.' The two moved towards the dais and as they did so Kirsten's legs felt as if they would give way. Her throat tightened and she clenched her hands, digging her nails hard into the palms of her hands. Again her hand drifted to the Brooch and she clasped it firmly. Hundreds of eyes bored into the back of her head and she felt her face and neck burn.

For a long time the old man looked at her, his piercing eye penetrating hers, until she could take no more and looked away.

'Choan, Whott is the meaning of thiss?' he hissed. 'Who und whott is thiss? Yow know the laws of this lund und of strangchers.'

Choan stood tall and looked straight at the Mullach. 'Oh mighty wun, it wuss a mistake of my kinsmen who tuke this gurrl when they werr searching forr anumuls in the high lands. This gurrl came upon my kinsmen and saw them. They hud no choice butt to take hurr, forr she wude have spoken.'

'Fools!' he bellowed, 'This us badd! Yow know the laws.'

'We know, butt we werr trapped unto this. Oh mighty Mullach, whott us to be dunn?'

For a long time the old man did not speak. He rolled the green stone that hung around his neck in his palm and thought. Then he tapped the stone dais with his finger and addressed Choan. 'Yow have brought this problem hither. This gurrl must now stey wuth yowr family. She cannagt be allowed back to her laand, forr she wull tell and yow know the laws. Thiss iss my judgement.'

Kirsten gasped uttered a half audible cry and fainted.

When she came back to her senses, she found herself stretched out on the rock beside Choan and his family at the edge of the assembly. A swelling chant arose once more from the crowd as the Mullach walked around the dais and raised the green stone in his hands, before all the people. Kirsten could not believe that she was condemned to remain here, forever. She wanted to cry but found, now that her sudden misery was turning to anger, that her eyes were dry. How dare they keep her here. The Mullach held up the green stone and as he did so it caught in the blue light and sent a cascade of green sparkles around the cavern. 'The Orbed-time uss now near-times and ut wull soon be time forr the keeping famuly to brung the blue stone.'

Kirsten was immediately aware of Choan gasping and crying out under his breath. She could not make it out. 'Choan, yowr famuly huv been the keeping famuly this lasst time. Yow wull brung the stone tow me soon-times.'

Choan raised himself reluctantly to his feet and looked appallingly pale in the eerie blue glow of he cave. 'Yess, oh Mullach,' he said falteringly, 'We wull brring the blue stone tow the meeting att the Orbed-time. Owr famuly has keept the stone well forr menny generations.' His words meant little to Kirsten, but they seemed hollow and unconvincing. Whatever Choan was saying he was lying and afraid.

Nor was this lost upon the Mullach who looked at him with his piercing slatey eyes and spoke. 'Yess yow wull brring it here at the Orbed-time. Yow arre the keeper und we wull celebrate together. We wull see if the time is right forr owr people tow return tow our home.' The Mullach was suspicious and Choan looked more uncomfortable than ever. A complete silence fell upon the gathering. No one spoke or grunted, and all held their breaths. The Mullach, his eyes glaring, leapt up and swung his hand around his head twice, then descended from the dais and swept off with his retinue out of the dell.

Kirsten saw sweat trickle in running beads down Choan's face and from the corner of her eye recognised the sneering, jeering, smirking form of the wiry Morlech. Choan's family all looked unsettled; Crallogh was trembling, Urick was as pale as a full moon. Kirsten looked at these things, seeing but not understanding. Her situation seemed more hopeless than ever.

Chapter 9

The Opportunity

Choan stood facing the scrawny form of Morlech. He had him by the neck and was waving his cudgel threateningly in his face. Morlech looked at him with contempt as Choan shook him and cried out, 'Wherre is the blue Orbed, Morlech? Tell me wherre is utt yow wretch?' He was shouting fiercely, fury burning in his eyes. Kirsten was afraid to see him in this mood. 'Yow said thut yow would cause disaster tow fall up onto owr famuly and yow have dun it. Yow wull answer tow me for this. Dow yow hear me wurm? Where is the blue Orbed? – If yow do nagt guv ut tow me I wull wrung yowr neck.'

With a writhing twist Morlech worked himself free and spat sneeringly in Choan's face. 'Yow do-nagt know where the Blue Orbed is?' he said sarcastically. 'Hah! Yow wull die then wull yow nagt. Hagh Hagh! For I do-nagt know. Hagh Hagh!' He smirked showing a set of rotten, stained teeth. He was enjoying seeing the dread in Choan's face. 'Hagh! Hagh!'

'Yow lie!' bellowed, Choan, 'Yow know.'

'Oh na. I do-nagt. Yow are the keeper are yow nagt?,' he said mockingly. 'So the keeper musst have the stone. Yow hud better have the stone dow yow nagt think?' He stabbed the air in front of Choan with his finger, taunting him. Choan made to grab him again.

'Yow know, Morlech yow filthy ragbat!' But Morlech was slinking off casting derisive jeers back at Choan as he ran, laughing. Choan slammed the cudgel fiercely into the palm of his hand and stood looking after the shrinking form of Morlech, shaking – with fear and rage. Now he turned to his family and spoke. 'This is a badd time forr owr famuly. Never hav we been un such danger und I do nagt know whott tow do. Yow heard the swine – he says he hus nagt gott the Orbed – butt who else cann have ut?'

One of the women, the one who had tried to befriend Kirsten, spoke up, her voice wailing like an angry seagull. 'I can nagt believe that this hass happened. How dud the stone go mussing, Choan? How coulld ut? Yow had ut in our posset of precious thungs had not yow? Yow always had ut safe.'

'Yes, Aros,' agreed Choan. 'But ut was hiddenn und I do nagt know how ut has come to pass thus wyse. The Mullach wunts ut at the time of the nexst full light. I feared he wud wunt tow see ut thus council time, butt when I went to fetch ut before-times I could nagt find ut. I hoped he might nott ask tow see ut when we had Churstun to fill his mind – he might have forgotten ut – He nearly did, butt I thunk he susspects. The Mullach always founds out owr wrong-doings. There is no baddness that can be hud frum him. But he demands to huv it soon or we wull be punished.'

'Yow musst find ut then, orr yow wull be culled,' sobbed the woman.

'Yes, I know, we musst,' said Choan, dejectedly, 'und we huv to be keepers of Churstun.'

A snort came from the middle of the small crowd, and their heads turned towards Urick, who tossed his head. 'Hagh! We have had nuthing but trubble sunce Crallogh brought Churstun to here. Why shude we nagt be rid of herr. She is nuthing tow uss.' As he spoke his upper lip curled and his nostrils flared like an angry horse. The cold blue light of his eye was like an icy dart as he cast a look at Kirsten who shrank back and shivered. 'We have na reason tow want to take carre of her, we musst be rid of her. What saye yow all?'

A general hubbub of approval arose from the rest of the group. The fear they had about their predicament had driven out all concern they had had for Kirsten's well-being. Even Aros seemed to agree.

'Yes!' they cried, 'We wull be rid of her. Bind her und we wull cast herr intow the blue lochan.' The group closed round her and Kirsten felt the iron grip of Crallogh close around her wrists and the tight snare of a cord, once more being slipped over them. Then came a shove in her back and she fell to the ground hitting her head fiercely on the stone floor. She tried to utter a scream through her dry, cracked lips, but only a half-stifled, cracked whine came out.

'No! No! please no, I will stay and help you. Please no! No!' Still the group pressed around her. She saw the menacing look of Crallogh and in Urick's eye a hint of pleasure. The women were cursing and spitting at her and even the few children kicked her shins and prodded their hard fingers into her ribs. Closer they drew until the hot smell of their stinking breath was in her face. No one would ever know what had become of her. She knew now that her fate had come.

'Nagt! NAGT!' The group hesitated, then halted in their action as the sound of the cry rose and fell echoing off the roof of the cavern. From a distance the crashing sound of the cold river came as the water tumbled in its fall to dash itself upon the rocks, by the cave. Nothing else could be heard. The crowd was, for that moment, silent and still. But the halt lasted scarcely a few seconds for then the crowd, hungry with the scent of blood moved again, shoving the girl to her knees. 'NAGT! NAGT! I said, NAGT!'

This time the halt was complete and all eyes turned to the point where Choan stood upon a rock, his hand holding his cudgel raised high above his head. The light of the lochan cast a shadow from beneath him upon the roof of the cavern where his outline in giant form looked a hundred times more fearsome. 'NAGT! I have promussed the Mullach tow care forr Churstun. Whot do yow thunk wull happen iff she is harmed? She is un owr care. Do yow nagt thunk that he wull have even more reason tow punnish uss? She us owr only hope of having his anger stayed. Leave her I say,' he cried. The crowd wavered, unsure. Choan looked around them all and continued, 'Butt the stone we musst find the stone before the Orbed-time at the bugg light.'

'Hagh!' grunted Urick. 'She is trubble. Yow wull be wrong father. Yow wull regrett thiss.'

Unwillingly, the group fell back, one by one, leaving Kirsten quivering on the ground.

Some hours later Choan searched Kirsten out. She was still shaken and suspicious. 'Yow wull be safe now,' he said, ' I have seen tow that.'

'I do not know, Choan. How can I trust you?' she sobbed.

'Churstun, I will see to ut that yow wull be safe, forr my people can nagt hurt yow when I am here. Trusst me.'

Kirsten looked at him disbelievingly. Perhaps three or four days had passed since she had fallen from her own real, safe, loving caring world into this nightmare life where she was so out of place, in so much danger. All she could think was that she was condemned to live here miserably for the rest of her life, however short that was likely to be. She faced up to Choan and said bitterly, 'I suppose I have to trust you Choan, don't I? I have no choice.' He looked at her with a knitted brow and kept silent. Kirsten watched him lost in his thoughts. 'Choan,' she ventured eventually, 'You seem to think you may be in danger yourself. What help can you be to me then?'

Choan looked at her uncomfortably. He said nothing. 'Please, Choan, answer me. You say I'm to be in your family. Well tell me what is this trouble that you are in? What is the Blue Orbed and why were you shouting at Morlech, and why was he looking so satisfied? Tell me, Choan, tell me!'

Choan leaped to his feet and began to pace to and fro, thumping his thigh with his fist. 'The Blue Orbed...' he said, 'the Blue Orbed is the secund of the preciouss stones, the twinn stones of the Pixsts. The grreen stone und the blue stone. Yow saw the grreen stone this meeting time. Ut was around the neck of the Mullach. Grreen like the moss of the meadow un owr wurld, shaped like the eggg of a burrd. The blue stone us jusst the ssame – only blue, wuth a circle around ut at one end. They are preciouss tow the people forr they are used at Orbed-time tow tell whether the time is right. Oh so preciouss. The grreen stone is great, butt the blue stone is greaterr. Ut wull tell the time.'

Kirsten could hardly follow Choan's meaning, but listened patiently. He was very agitated and pacing up and down as he spoke. 'Each session the Blue Orbed is gaven tow one famuly tow keep. The Mullach always keeps the twinn stone, but when he calls forr ut, the blue stone must be brott. To lose ut means that all the angerr of the people wull be against the famuly. Und ut is losst. I went tow find ut where we kepe ut, butt ut was gone. We arre lost tow.'

Choan stopped and looked at the girl. He had thought she would be looking afraid, or sad or in despair. Yet she was not. A glow was in her eyes which were wide and alert. 'Choan,' she said, I think I have seen the stone. I'm sure I have.'

'Graggh!' the other snorted.

'I mean it, Choan. I'm sure I have seen it. It is dark

blue, deep, deep blue, a white line curving round it, slightly rough and shaped just about this big.' She cupped her hand to a size that would have accommodated a large hen's egg.

Now it was his turn to look at her in wonder, a vague hope in his eyes. 'Wherre?' he demanded, shortly.

'On the beach, my beach near my village.'

'Nagt! Dow nagt trick me, Churstun.'

'I am not tricking you, Choan. I mean it. It is true. One day I found a stone on the beach just as I described to you. It sparkles gently in the light...'

'Huggg!' he exclaimed, but he was listening.

'...and a sort of dimple at one end, a dent about the size of a tooth.'

He swung round suddenly and faced her. 'Yah! That is ut!' he cried. 'But tell me now-times, wuth now lying, wherre dud yow see ut, Churstun?'

'It is as I said, Choan, it was on the beach near my village.'

He grabbed her by the shoulders and shook her fiercely. 'I dow nagt beleeve yow! Yow have seen ut hereby sum-time. All yow want is tow try unde escape tow your world. Yow arr making ut upp. Yow musst have seen ut herby sumtime.'

'I am not,' pleaded the girl.

He released her grip and a dark look spread over his brow once more. Half under his breath he muttered, 'Yow musst be lying, Chursten, I can-nagt thunk how ut wude gett tow the high lands.'

'Yah! She musst be.' The voice was sharp and sudden.

Kirsten wheeled round. It was Urick, a malicious look on his face. He was standing legs apart looking at his father. 'Dow nagt trusst her father. She wull be tellung us lies. Yow are right. All she is wunting is tow escape. I thunk that she hass takenen the stone und hidden ut sumwhere. She lies! She lies!'

Choan looked convinced by Urick's words and turned on the girl once more. 'Tell me, Churstun, wherre huv yow poot the stone? Remember yow arre in my care. If yow do nagt tell me then we might us well casst yow unto the lochan now-times. Tell me now, Churstun.' He took her by the shoulders, and looked straight into her eyes.

How could she convince him it was true? Kirsten held his gaze and looked straight back, deep into the recesses of his sapphire blue eyes without flinching. Then quite calmly she spoke, 'It is as I said, Choan, it was on the beach near my village.'

The two stood looking at each other. The man penetrating and searching her and the girl resolutely holding his gaze, never flinching, never blinking just waiting. At last he nodded slowly. 'Yah, I thunk thut yow musst be tellung the truth. There is na lie un yowr eyes, Churstun. Though how ut came tow be owt of owr care und in the high lands I do nagt know.'

There was a noise from behind him. 'Nagt, father, ut musst be hudden hereby sumwhere by the gurrl.'

'Nagt, yow arre wrong, Urick. I trusst her. Mayhaps Morlech has casst ut there tow try und brung us trubble.' The boy said no more. 'Butt how are we tow find ut now-times?'

Kirsten kept her peace and waited. She ached inside, she knew what she wanted to suggest, she knew that this was her only hope for an opportunity of escape from this awful place and yet she knew that the decision, the direction and the plan had to come from Choan, himself.

She waited and it was like waiting for someone to catch you and break your fall when you have stumbled. Would he hold out the chance to her or not? It seemed to her that her life was held in the balance of that moment. One word from Urick might sway Choan from the direction she needed him to take. Equally, one word from her might reawaken his suspicions and turn him away from her.

Choan deliberated for what seemed a very long time, staring at his knuckles as he contemplated. And then he looked up and spoke.

'Churstun,' he said, 'I have na hope unless yow wull take the tassk tow find the Blue Orbed. We have tow trusst yow. If yow fail I musst surely die. If yow succeed then yow musst be given the greatest honourr umung owr people.'

'Nagt!' came a half startled, stifled gasp from the lips of Urick. He looked afraid, alarmed.

'Yah!' snapped Choan. 'I have decided. Yow musst go tow the high lands and brung back the stone. Ut is tow dangerous forr us tow go un case we were seeen. Butt if yow go, Churstun, yow can brung me the stone.' He looked hopeful and the look of fear and desperation that had been haunting his face ever since the council with the Mullach began to fade at last. 'We wull plan tow gett yow there verry soon.'

Kirsten bit into her lip with joy. She would be free.

Chapter 10

The Hidden Journey

Once he had made up his mind Choan was spurred to rapid action. He called the rest of his family around him at the threshold of the stone homestead. They clustered around his feet, fifteen in all, and listened silently as he outlined his plan. Kirsten could not interpret the look upon their faces. They were set as stone, and none of them spoke save an occasional grunt from Crallogh. Urick, cast his usual evil look at her, but remained silent until Choan had finished. Then a disagreement arose – clearly they were not behind Choan. Kirsten, who had been forced to sit a little distance off could not quite hear the debate but gathered that they were concerned only for the safety and the recovery of the blue stone. At length Choan motioned to her to join them and gave his final decision.

'I um reddy now-times tow do whott musst be dun. I wull leave frum here and sett off, as uff I am going tow the farr lands beyond Rum.' Again Kirsten was amazed to hear a name that she recognised. How far *did* this world extend? Choan continued, 'Yow wull tell Morlech und hus people thut we are going un search of the stone und make sure that he does nagt follow uss. Churstun wull look furr the stone where she says ut us tow be found, though how ut came tow be on the high lands I can-nagt tell. We leave nexst meal time.'

And so it was that a few hours later, Choan, Crallogh and Kirsten set off, the men wearing their large round boots and Kirsten trotting beside them to keep up with their pace. They headed initially in the direction of the meeting dell.

As they walked they passed Morlech crouching over a dead rat, a black, large, red-eyed, creature. He was skinning the animal. When he saw the group his horrendous face twisted into a sneering grimace. 'Hagh! Yow wull nagt huv long, Choan. Yow are on the wrung foot. Hagh! Hagh! Hagh!' His words gurgled in his throat like the hoarse laugh of a braying donkey. The rest of his family gathered around Morlech and leant upon each other laughing, jeering and sneering.

Choan and Crallogh cast them hardly a glance, but turned and skirted the ridge of the small hillock that hid the dell from view. They kept then to the highest points staying in full view of a number of dwelling circles, scattered around the great cavern. From this vantage point Kirsten was able to see, for the first time, that a number of tunnels opened in the walls of the cavern near the dell, and tracks were worn into the moss and rocky scrub of the floor such that all of them offered upon the centre of the dell like the spokes of a wheel. She understood that this must be a central meeting point, the spot where all roads converged. She could see too that the roof of the dell formed an almost circular canopy, rising to a point, all clustered with glistening rock, sparkling faintly in the blue light of the place.

Choan halted and cast a long look around the cavern. What was he doing? He stood and looked in all directions and as he did so it slowly dawned upon Kirsten that the eyes of all those in the nearer parts of the cavern were upon him. He was making himself as visible and obvious as possible. Then quite deliberately he selected one of the openings in the wall of the cave and strode off into its dark mouth. Crallogh gave Kirsten a shove on the shoulder and she too followed, while he brought up the rear.

The passage was wide, and as they walked the general blue iridescence faded. As it did so Kirsten was conscious that the rocks themselves still appeared to glow, although they did so with much less intensity than the shimmering lochan. There was enough light to walk by and enough even to make out the structure of the walls and floor. Here in this dim light, Kirsten could see carved into the walls, the shapes of men, beasts and landscapes. There were cows, boars, birds, fish and the faces of many men – stone men – with their square jaws and pleated beards.

At one point she stopped dead in her tracks. On a flat rock face was carved in relief a sight she knew well. There on the stone wall, unmistakably, was the Carraig cliff, the outline of Muck and the Sgurr of Eigg. It was the view from the beach, her beach. A wave of desperation and longing swept over her. All she wanted was to see that view again, for real.

Choan halted and looked at her. 'The high lands,' he said. 'Thutt is the land off my people. Thutt is whare we werr driven fromm. Ut is owr land und we would gow bagck there uf we could, we wull sum time.'

'Choan, that is my land, that is my beach.'

'Nagt!'

'It is, Choan. It is the place where I am happiest.' He grunted irritably and scowled. 'Choan,' continued Kirsten appealingly, ' that is where I saw the blue stone. I promise you.'

He regarded her again, stonily, and then set off at a great pace. 'We musst moove fasst orr we wull be duscuvered.'

Again Crallogh gave Kirsten a dig and she set off running to catch up Choan. They seemed to travel for miles, turning along passages, climbing steps or squeezing through almost impassable cracks in the rock. From time to time Kirsten heard voices or the quiet pad of bare feet upon stone. Choan would pull the others into a deep crack and there they would sit in utter, silence, holding their breath until the noise had faded. Kirsten could not work out what direction they were following, but had the distinct impression they were travelling around in circles. She estimated that they must have covered twelve miles or more, before she sank to her knees and called out pitifully, 'Choan, stop! I cannot go any further.'

'Yow musst! Ut is nagt farr now-times.'

'I cannot go another step,' she moaned.

Again he looked at her, almost tenderly, and bent down. He took her by the arm and quickly slung her, stomach down, over his shoulder. 'We musst hurry. There is nagt eny time tow spare.' And so he lolled off swinging Kirsten over his shoulder, knocking the wind out of her.

Crallogh had gone on ahead and now came hurrying back. 'Thiss way,' he hissed, 'Morlech may bee abowt.'

Kirsten heard Choan utter something under his breath as he darted up a tunnel. They lay against the flat wall of a small recess almost hidden by a boulder. Kirsten could just see the main passage twenty feet away. Three figures stopped and sniffed the air.

'I susspect Choan,' said one.

'Yes, I am surre, Morlech thut he is upp tow trubble. Ut wull be a greatt thung forr uss iff we can brung this great disusterr uppon him. Hagh!'

'Yuss, Slingish!' came the rasping cursing tones of Morlech himself. 'Butt I sense that Choan is sumwhere nearr und is doing something wuth the gurrl. We musst try und find owt und tell the Mullach. Thenn where wull Choan be?'

This was greeted with a chorus of gurgling, gasping, coughing guffaws the hollowness of which frightened Kirsten more than any sound she had heard since she had left her home on the night she fell into this crazy dream. The three figures stood still at that spot for a long time, resting, sniffing the air like dogs and listening. Choan signalled to Kirsten to keep absolutely still, and this she did until her muscles ached and her feet had gone numb from doing so.

At length the three searchers moved off, but still Choan sat motionless. Kirsten opened her mouth to whisper a question to him but as quickly as she had done so, she found his hand clasped firmly over it as a gag. Again he signalled to her to remain absolutely still. The pain in her legs and cramped feet was now almost unbearable, but suddenly this was forgotten, for there again at the mouth of the small hollow, stood Morlech sniffing and gazing intently right to the spot where she sat. Fortunately Kirsten was in the shadow and after some more minutes Morlech kicked his foot against a rock and shambled off. Only when he had been absent for quarter of an hour or more did Choan and Crallogh rest their tightened muscles.

'Curse him! Ut is hus way. He always cumms back tow be sure. I knew he would cumm back tow chechk this spott againn. Und curse him forr he hus brott dususter onn owr famuly. Dud yow nott hear ut fromm hus own lups!'

'Ya!' croaked Crallogh. 'Yowr plann hud better wurk, Choan.'

Kirsten was trying to rub some sensation back into her aching limbs. She was weary, and in pain, but now that she sensed her opportunity to escape was near at hand she was hardly aware of these troubles.

Choan led off again and they presently began to ascend a set of rough stone cut steps. Kirsten had a sense of familiarity about this spot. Surely they must have passed it already in this long, exhausting journey. The passage then led along a gently rising incline and with a sudden start Kirsten felt a cool chill blow upon her face.

At last! Fresh air funnelling into the dark space. And just audible were the sound of waves crashing on rocks. Her heart began to beat loudly and violently in her breast. As they walked on the sounds became ever louder, ever more homely and soon she could make out the ululating call of seagulls on the wind.

Choan halted and pushed Kirsten onto a rock to sit. They were on the ledge high in the crack of the great cleft of the Carraig Cliffs, where Kirsten had first entered the land of the stone men. It was dark night outside, and a faint wisp of moonlight was all that prodded in to the depths of the cave. Kirsten could hear bats buzzing and diving and smelt and tasted salt in the air.

Choan now looked at her full in the face fixing her with a severe look and frowning. 'Yow, Churstun, arr parrt of owr famuly now-times. Yow know I musst have the Blue Stone orr the Mullach will nagt allow me tow live. Yow say ut is on yowr beach. Yow musst find utt, and return now. Yow have only one meals distance tull yow musst be back. I wull wait here, Crallogh will go with you.'

Kirsten saw her chance of escape vanish before her eyes. How could she escape if Crallogh were to go with her? 'Choan,' she said desperately, 'It is dark. I cannot hope to look for the stone in the dark.'

'Yow musst. Yow said yow knew where it was.'

'Yes I did. But there are thousands of stones on the beach. It is lying there among them. I would need the full light of day to look and even then it would take me a long time,' she reasoned.

'Yow do nagt huv a long time!'

'I cannot look without the big light.'

'But then Crallogh could nagt go with yow, orr he might be seen. We huv enough trubble wuth the Mullach than tow be seen un the high lands.'

'Hagh!' exclaimed Crallogh. 'Dud I nagt tell yow,

Choan, thut she would jusst try und escape. Yow are a fool, Choan.'

Choan turned on the other stone man angrily and shook him fiercely by the arm. 'But owr only hope of finding the Blue Stone is tow send Churstun. Do yow nagt thunk I know the dangerr if she does not returrn to us. Yow heard Morlech. He wull make sure thut the Mullach learns of it und eny hope I have wull be losst – nagt just me but owr whole famuly. Yow too.'

He hesitated for a moment and furrowed his heavy brow. 'I musst know who took the Orbed,' he said, a wild look in his eyes. 'Thatt mann wull surely die. Ut musst have been Morlech and we arr going tow show the Mullach thatt. I need the stone und I need the prooff of his guilt. When we have that owr famuly will be safe again.' He turned once more to Kirsten. There was a look of desperation now in his eyes. He needed the girl and he needed to trust her, yet he was not sure that he could do so. If he lost the stone, he would surely be killed on the Mullach's orders, if he lost Kirsten, then the word of the Mullach would go against his family too. 'How long wull ut take yow, Churstun?'

Kirsten tried to be realistic. 'It might take years.' Choan leapt up fiercely growling. 'But maybe only months or days if I am lucky...' she added hastily.

'Days?' queried Choan, a puzzled look on his face. 'How meny tides is thut?'

Tides? Kirsten was confused too for a moment. Then she realised that in the world of constant light where the stone men lived there was no day, or night. They talked only of the light and dark of the high lands. 'Fourteen or fifteen tides... seven or eight big lights.'

Choan leapt down from his perch and swung himself down the rock face and onto the floor of the cave. He was gone for two or three minutes and then returned swinging himself noiselessly up the rock face to the ledge once more. 'I have seen the luttle light. It is beyond the half. Yow have fourteen tides at the most. Yow must dow ut.'

'Nagt!' expostulated Crallogh. 'Yow musst not let her go alone. She wull nevverr returrn.'

'She wull go, and she wull returrn,' answered Choan firmly. 'I wull trusst her tow do ut.'

'Yow fooll Choan.'

'Churstun,' said Choan, addressing her directly once more, 'Yow wull go und look. Yow musst return wuth the stone. Uf yow do nagt, be sure the people of my land wull be overr yowr land too, like the Pixts were driven off past times ago. Every luttle light I wull be here und see, I wull have a rope here forr yow tow climb back up. Do nagt fail me. The Mullach wull want the Blue Stone at the Orbed-time which is when the luttle light is round.'

He looked at her so intently and earnestly that Kirsten could hardly hold his gaze. She did not utter a word, she dare not, but looked blankly back. She was not going to promise him anything. All she wanted was to feel the rounded pebbles of the shore outside the caves under her feet, feel the wind in her hair, and see the moon riding high over the peaks of Rum.

Choan swung her onto his shoulder once more and clambered down the rock face to the floor of the cave. Her heart was singing joyously in her chest. 'Go now und do nagt fail me, Churstun,' croaked Choan. She turned towards the gap in the cleft of rock where the moonlight was shining in silver dapples upon a tossing sea and walked out of the cave. She was free.

From the hollow depths of the great cleft she heard the despairing call of Crallogh to his leader, 'Fooll! Fooll! Fooll!'

'Fool indeed!' thought Kirsten, to herself, 'Yes, fool indeed!'

Chapter 11

Recovery

Kirsten made her way along the shore slowly at first. She did not want to arouse Choan's suspicions by being too hasty as she walked and picked her way carefully over the jagged, rocky outcrops in the moonlight. She wanted to run, run as fast as her legs would carry her, to the familiar safety of her home, where her family would be together, lying asleep and a dying fire would lie in the grate. The air was chill and she could hardly suppress the desire to shout out loud with joy. Above her in a cloudless sky an oval moon rode and the black of the heavens was sown with a tapestry of stars. There was just enough light to allow her to pick her way.

Still she could hardly believe that she was free. All she had to do was to reach the security of the croft and she would be safe at last. She was aware of Choan's eyes, watching her every step and held her composure and her pace until she was past the first of the small, sandy coves and well out of his sight. Then she could bear it no longer and broke into a run. She stumbled and ran over the rough ground, leaping over rocks at a dangerous pace. She wanted to put as much space between her and the cave as she could.

On she bounded, plunging recklessly through squelching bogs and over treacherously slippy rocks. Thistles and thorny branches of some low scrubby bushes caught in her hair and tore a rent in her shawl, but she did not care, she could almost smell the familiar odour of her home. Ahead was a puddle in a clump of wet moss and she took a great leap over it to a darker shadow which she thought was a large slab of rock.

But in the pale light her eyes had deceived her. This was no rock. The dark shadow beyond the mossy sward was a cleft in the ground itself. Suddenly Kirsten felt herself flailing wildly in space, her legs kicking and thrashing, and then she was tearing through a clump of gorse, slowing her fall, until her head crashed hard against rock and she remembered nothing more.

'Jamie, I think we should be looking at the shoreline again,' said Sandy flatly.

'Yes,' sighed his brother in law, ' I suppose we must.' His brown, friendly face was worn with concern and a dejected stoop had taken its place on his usually broad shoulders. 'Perhaps this tide will have brought her ashore.' His voice was very flat and depressed. 'I cannot bear to think of her lost forever. Who knows where the currents will carry her to. She could even have been carried as far as the islands.'

An unbearably deep sadness had now fallen upon all the croft folk. Six full days had passed since Kirsten's disappearance and everyone knew that she must be dead. Only Jessie clung on with a mother's undying hope, that her daughter might yet be found safe – and Jamie's practical words had been dismissed. Even Sandy, had given up any real hope of finding her body, but he pressed his brother in law to continue the search. They had to be doing something.

After their supper the two men wandered aimlessly down to the shore by Kirsten's beach in silence. There was nothing they felt like saying to each other, but both walked keeping company only with their thoughts. Jamie was worried as to how Jessie would ever come to terms with the loss of her daughter. Sandy would have given anything to stay at the croft for as long as he could, but he knew that in a few short weeks he would have to set off for Glasgow and rejoin his ship.

They looked half-heartedly as they walked over this ground they had covered so often in the last few days. There was no sign – they did not really expect to see any. At the beach they parted, Jamie doubling back to work the shore towards Sanna, Sandy concentrating his search along the coastline towards the Carraig Cliffs.

He had seen troubles of all kinds in his travels around the globe, and had even lost several men riding out a typhoon in the Indian Ocean, when the waves had been higher than a church steeple. But in this place, his home, tragedies like this did not happen. It was a place of peace and rest, not of disaster and loss. He was more unhappy and resigned as each moment passed, but still he would look – for Jessie's sake.

In this frame of mind he approached the head of a small, green sward where the bracken gave way to a stretch of tangled and thorny gorse before tumbling off in broken, jagged boulders to a gully. He had been at this spot a dozen times in the last few days and seen nothing. The sun was falling, crimson red into the sea, the air was still as a whisper and at any other time he would have rejoiced at the sight.

Now clouds of midgies danced around him crawling through his hair and beard, irritating him furiously as they bit. He shook his head in a bad temper, and swung his arms around testily, cursing the tiny creatures. But as he did so a gleam just caught the corner of his eye, from further up the dell. In the next moment he lost it. The sun was now very low and would soon be so low that that spot would be lost in the shadow of a rock, and so he twisted and squinted wildly trying to gain sight of it again. At last he succeeded in catching the tiny, dazzling gleam again and, marking the spot against a stone and a bush, worked his way to the point.

For a full half hour he crawled among the bracken and the gorse going over the same ground, countless times. The grass was long and tussocky and every movement he made disturbed the surface, sending further armies of midgies to wage war against him until his eyes, his ears and his cheeks burned with discomfort and pain.

He was about to surrender and retreat when his hand fell upon something hard in the grass and as his hand closed round it his heart gave a leap. Sandy pulled the object free and looked down. There, in his palm, glowing warmly in the last rays of a dying sun, lay the Kerala brooch, a golden crescent with a blue stone set in it. Kirsten had been here! It told him nothing more than that. He could not even say when she had been at the spot, but at last there was something.

Now in a deepening gloaming he began to search the ground in ever widening circles. The light was fading and the midgies were attacking him relentlessly, giving him no quarter. At last he found another sign, a small twist of plaid caught on a bramble bush above a deep, hollow crevasse. He squinted in the dim light and caught a glimpse of something he could hardly believe. It was difficult to be sure, but lying almost completely hidden by a tangle of gorse and brambles he thought he saw the twisted hump of a body. Desperately he climbed down into the depths of that pit until he had reached it – the motionless, lifeless body of Kirsten.

The commotion at the croft house was great. All the villagers had arrived in the doorway, white-faced and shocked after Sandy had stumbled into the hamlet with Kirsten slung over his shoulder. At the sight of her lifeless body Jessie collapsed in sobs.

94

'No wait! Wait, Jessie!' soothed Sandy. 'She is not dead, not yet. Somehow she is still alive, though how I will never know. But look to the wound on her head. It is deep and she has lain unconscious a long, long time. I fear it will take her a long time to recover. If ever,' he added under his breath.

In the delirious joy that followed this discovery Sandy recounted the story of the brooch and the exact spot where he had just caught sight of her foot through the tangle of scrub. 'How we missed her before now I'll never know,' he said. 'We must have been at that spot ten times or more. It was just the brooch that did it, and that by a trick of the light.'

Jessie bathed her head and as she did so Kirsten opened her eyes briefly and smiled weakly. 'Mother,' she said and then lapsed back into unconsciousness.

For the next two days Kirsten was so weak and fevered that all still feared for her recovery. She had lain unconscious at the bottom of the ravine for almost a day and was now suffering greatly. The rest, of course, assumed that she had lain there since her disappearance almost a week earlier, and blessed the fact that the weather had been warm and dry; or else, as Macphail had unhelpfully reminded Jessie, she would have died of the cold long ago.

Her head ached terribly and she remembered little of what was going on around her. In her dreams Kirsten saw stone men, chanting before the Mullach in the great cavern, chasing her, tying her arms behind her back drawing her back, deep into the bowels of the earth, and she screamed out loud in fear. They were black dreams and her family could make out little of her rantings when she cried aloud.

It was Jessie's turn to be tireless now, as she mopped

her daughter's brow and poured sips of warm milk into her dry chapped lips. She had her back and despite her frailty Kirsten was safe under their roof at last.

On the second day, Kirsten woke quite suddenly from her sleep and sat upright in bed. 'Mother, I am very hungry. Can I have something to eat, please?' Her eyes were clear, her temperature settled to normal and Jessie heaved a deep sigh, thanking God that Kirsten was home, recovered. The crisis was passed – all would be well.

'Oh Yes! Yes, my dear,' she said and busied herself instantly in preparing some food for the girl.

From that moment, Kirsten's recovery seemed both miraculously quick and surprisingly complete. How could someone lie for almost a week, at the bottom of a twenty foot drop, having knocked themselves uncon-scious, and not only survive, but recover so rapidly? It was incomprehensible, but everyone rejoiced and were delighted when after only another couple of days she was running about the croft, her usual self, fetching, carrying and playing with the others. Her recovery was indeed complete.

No one said anything about her disappearance on the night that McKinnon's bull had also gone missing, and Kirsten for her part said only (and quite truthfully) that she could remember nothing of her fall, or how she came to be at the bottom of the ravine. However, in her dreams she still saw stone men, rising to pursue her and she often cried out about them in her sleep, or woke shaking. Jessie and Jamie could make nothing of her ravings and put it down to the knock on the head. By day it was just so wonderful to be back in her own home that she said nothing of it herself, but concentrated on dismissing it from her mind. Whenever the dark thoughts came into her head she fixed her thoughts on something much more real and pleasant. In time she would be able to forget the awful experience. It would remain nothing more than a bad dream. Or so she thought.

What did she care for the stone men? They had taken her, captured her and held her in that frightful place under the ground. Among the hills and with the smells of the bog myrtle, the peat and the sea in her nostrils she cared for nothing but living freely with her family.

She was an ever willing help to Jessie, who jokingly observed that the 'Dunt on her head had done her nothing but good.' When Hughie complained about something she threatened to mete the same injury upon him in the hope he too would mend his ways. Jessie was overjoyed to have Kirsten back and Sandy visited often, beaming at her, but always with a curious look in his eye. He could not understand how he could have missed her at that spot, before. He was sure he had looked into it on several occasions. Kirsten must have moved or crawled some distance into better view.

As she lay in her bed he told her wild tales of his adventures on the sea; racing against the winds off the Cape; the time he nearly sailed into a war in East Africa where the tribes were fighting, but he found her less attentive than usual. She had a far away look and he trailed off. But Kirsten was listening even if her mind was drawn to another tribe of people.

Jessie soon settled back to a life of busy contentment and life began to take on a more normal air around the village.

It was one evening, perhaps six days after Kirsten's rescue by Sandy. She was sitting on a small hillock in the sand dunes down at Sanna, watching Hughie setting a rabbit snare. It was a perfect night, calm and quiet. No one could remember an August that had been so hot and dry as this one had been. There was hardly a breath of wind, the air so still that she could hear the engines of a puffer several miles offshore as it ploughed its way to one of the islands with its cargo, from Glasgow. Apart from the wake of the boat there was not a ripple on the glassy sea and a few lazy cormorants were sitting on the small rocky islands in the bay.

Kirsten was happy, contentedly watching Hughie. She had often fished with him from the rocks or from their father's boat, but had never seen him setting a snare before. He worked at his task thirty yards or so off, where numerous rabbit holes opened into a series of grassy mounds. Presently he rejoined her and the two sat quite still, watching. It was gloriously peaceful and neither was in a hurry to return home.

Short, green grass covered the sandy hillocks of the dunes, giving way to spiky maram grass nearer the beach itself. After a time rabbits came out, sixty, maybe seventy of them and grazed and played. Kirsten watched enthralled as they bounded about, taking very little notice of the two of them as they sat, motionless. She had watched rabbits at play hundreds of times, yet she remained fascinated by them.

Hughie made a sudden, involuntary movement with his arm to wave off some midgies that were irritating him. As he did so the rabbits, started and darted to their burrows, to seek safety underground in their warren of sandy passages and tunnels. They scattered and ran and as they disappeared from sight Kirsten had a sudden and unwanted recollection of the tunnels of the stone men.

It was so clear in her minds eye, as if she were watching the actual scene unfold before her. She saw the Picts chased from this very grassy hillock into those dark, stony passages where they now lived. She heard the shouts of the fierce warriors from the sea. She saw the

Picts running, their children screaming, trying to escape, and she saw only a few – one family – survive. She did everything she could to try and drive the image from her mind. She thought of everyday things, the croft, the school, walking with Sandy on the beach – but the image would not go. Anger filled her. Why could she not forget all about the stone men? Why did should she think about these people? They meant nothing to her. At that moment Hughie rose to his feet, and as he did so a large rabbit bolted for the hole where Hughie had stretched the noose of wire and fixed it with a short stake. The wire caught the animal around the neck and it kicked wildly to break free, tightening it as it did so.

Again Kirsten's mind was filled with images. She resented them and attempted to drive them from her mind, but she was powerless to do so. She saw Choan's trusting, penetrating blue eyes as he had fixed her and charged her to help him before he had lowered her to the ground and her freedom. She heard the accusing and bitter call of Crallogh as he had called Choan a fool, for letting her go, and she thought of Choan condemned to die, putting his trust in her. The rabbit tugged hard and with a fierce and terrified pull broke the stake out of the ground and disappeared down the hole.

'Curse it!' cried Hughie. 'The thing has broken it. It was a real big one too. We could have had a rare pie with that. It was caught in the trap.'

Under her breath Kirsten groaned. She was not free at all. Nothing could help her escape from this image of Choan. He had trusted her and she had thought of nothing but her own freedom. He was caught like the rabbit in a trap – but he would not escape unless...

Again she tried to put it out of her head. She looked out to the west. Before, this had always seemed to be such a safe place. How she wished it was so again. Riding low on the horizon near the surface of the water was the clear orb of the moon. Kirsten looked at it and gasped, realising with a start that it was almost round, a near perfect circle, and she remembered Choan's parting words. With a sickening feeling she realised that tomorrow would be the night of the full moon.

Chapter 12

The Quest

It was just as well for Kirsten, that in the days following her rescue and recovery, her mother was so relieved to have her back, that she was willing to let her daughter do more or less as she wished.

Kirsten had spent a troubled night tossing in her bed shaking off fearful dreams until she finally fell asleep shortly before dawn. Only when the rest of the family were up and about their chores did Jessie bend over and shake the girl awake.

'Come on now Kirsten, you have slept past your breakfast and it's time to be helping me here.'

Kirsten came to with a start and leapt out of her bed. She could not waste a moment of this day. Within an hour most of her own chores and errands were completed and, having satisfied her mother, she was heading for the shore. She jogged over the ground, eager to get there as soon as she could and begin her search in earnest. She felt a heavy responsibility, but along with it a feeling of dread. What if she were unable to find the stone? What if she did? There was nothing in her mind at that moment except a desire to be about the task. That would give some purpose to her day. At least she could tell herself she had tried. As she approached the beach and crested the final hillock, giving her a first good view of it, Kirsten's steps suddenly faltered and she drew to a stumbling halt. She looked with wide eyed amazement for a moment, and then broke into a run, scrambling down the rocks at a reckless pace and onto the sand. It could not be possible! It must not be possible. Surely, her eyes must be deceiving her. But they were not.

All over the sand were the unmistakable padded imprints of the feet of stone men. The whole sandy beach was churned and twisted as the feet had walked back and forward over it. There were furrows, twists and churning swirls, but here and there the definite outline of those padded marks Kirsten now knew so well.

Kirsten felt a pang in her chest. Did this mean that Choan had given up waiting and had come looking himself? Maybe he had he found the stone, and if so would the stone men then carry out his threat to return and claim their land – the land of her family? For a moment Kirsten stood in utter despair and could not think straight. She did not know what to do but threw herself down on a rock and turned things over and over in her mind.

If the stone men had found the Blue Orbed, ought she not now go and warn the villagers that they might come? Would they? Or would they go back to live the way they always had, silent and hidden below the ground? Yet Kirsten knew that no one would believe her, even if she tried to tell them her story. They had rejoiced at her recovery, but more than once Sandy had looked at her wonderingly and observed that, 'Maybe the dunt on the head had knocked the sense out of her.' They would think her story wild and fantastical. Therefore, eventually she settled that she must look for the stone, herself; that at least was her duty – to Choan and to her own family. If it had already been found she could perhaps plead that she had done her best to look for it. If it were still lost then she might yet manage to rescue Choan herself.

To find one stone in a beach strewn with thousands is as easy as picking out one particular ant from the others in an anthill, or catching a specific sandeel in a shoal. Her eyes were mesmerised by the stones as they seemed to shift and change and swim before her. As she looked at them they appeared to swell and shrink. Backwards and forwards over and over again she walked around the spot where she thought she had seen Hughie throw the stone that day. She tried sifting stones into piles of different sizes, but soon gave up as she realised the sheer numbers of the stones on the beach. She stood and threw stones from a distance to see where or how they landed.

For hours Kirsten worked at this until her neck ached with looking down and her feet throbbed from the press of the pebbles and boulders upon them. All the time the tide was rising covering more and more of the beach – and as it rose, it covered and washed away all the tracks of the stone men once more. No one would ever know that they had walked on this beach it would once again be smooth and perfectly swept clean by the tide. But Kirsten knew that they had come and so she worked on.

After a time she was aware of someone standing a short distance off, leaning against a rock regarding her curiously. 'What are you doing Kirsten?' It was Malcolm McKinnon the boy from Plocaig, who accompanied Kirsten and Hughie to school.

Kirsten did not want to tell Malcolm anything. He was the jeering, dull, disbelieving kind who would only make fun of her if he heard her outlandish tale and rejoice in making her the laughing stock of the school. 'Just looking for stones,' she replied blandly.

'Stones!' he scoffed. 'Huh! There's plenty here then. Big ones, wee ones, grey ones, white ones, blue ones, greeny ones.' He spoke scornfully and gave a mocking laugh. 'What kind of stones, Kirsten?'

'Oh just round ones,' she said testily. She was cross at being disturbed. the last thing she wanted was Malcolm hanging around her beach when she was intent upon this task. 'I like round ones, smooth, round ones.' She turned her back on him and continued as if he were not there. He stood saying nothing but watched her with amusement. Kirsten turned to him, feeling that she had to say something more. 'I just like the feel of round ones – they are my favourite.'

'I like flat ones,' he answered her, 'better for throwing, you see. Skimming! Ten jumps or more if you get it just right. And if you throw it just upright they will hit the water with hardly a splash. A dead man's dive. Look I'll show you.' He took a flat stone and threw it, spinning, exactly perpendicular to the water. It hit the water with a hardly audible thud and disappeared with almost no plume of spray. For some minutes he repeated the trick, until satisfied that he had perfected the art.

Kirsten watched intrigued. She had never seen that particular trick before. 'But a round stone,' continued Malcolm gibingly, 'just makes a splash. That is boring and much less skilful.' He bent down and picked up another stone, larger and rounder than the others. Drawing his hand back behind his head he wound it into a throw. As he did so Kirsten cried out. For in his hand he was clutching a blue stone, egg shaped, glistening, the blue image of the stone she had seen hanging round the neck of the Mullach. The Blue Orbed! His hand flew forward, his fingers straightened releasing the stone in an upward curve that stretched out over the water of the bay. As it flew it rolled gently in the sunlight sending sparkles and small flashes from its surface, until it plummeted into the water with a tremendous splash and was hidden from sight as the water closed over it.

Kirsten called out fiercely, 'Why did you throw that stone, Malcolm. Not that stone! I wanted that stone.'

'It was only a stone, Kirsten,' answered the boy surprised by the venom in her voice. 'There are plenty of others on the beach.' And to emphasise the point he bent and picked up a beautifully polished white onyx, almost round and with a dark wave of colour arching through its surface.

It was a very beautiful stone but Kirsten ignored it. She stood rooted to the spot, anger, frustration and fear welling up in her. It had almost been in her hand, but now it was gone. She looked at the spot where widening ripples spread out from the point where it had hit the water, sixty feet out from the edge, and marked that spot by a dark shadow, where a weed-covered rock stood out from the yellow-green sea over the submerged sand of the bay. Kirsten stood disbelieving and in despair until Malcolm roused her. 'It was only a stone, Kirsten.'

There was nothing she could do. The stone was well out in the water. Too deep to swim for, or dive for. The tide was high and it would be a full six hours before it had gone right out. And so Kirsten retraced a weary route to the croft with Malcolm, who prattled on about this and that, while Kirsten, occupied with her own dark thoughts, ignored him.

A watched pot never boils and the tide never falls as rapidly as you expect if you are eager to see it flow out. Kirsten spent the rest of that day in a state of restless activity. She was working on a plan to be back at the beach at low tide, and had calculated that this would not be until about eight o'clock that night. No matter what she did she could not set her mind to it and worked half heartedly at everything else all that afternoon.

She thought of the footprints on the beach and all the time of Choan, who had trusted her, and who was now facing his judgement from the Mullach. This was a certainty now, for she knew that despite the footprints on the shore the Blue Orbed had not been found. It was as if time was running out on her and no matter how hard she tried to be patient she could not stop fretting. She would have to find some excuse to go to the shore but her mother would certainly make it difficult, for she still wanted Kirsten to rest early.

'Kirsten, you are looking very sombre,' observed Jamie at supper that evening. 'Are you feeling all right.'

'Yes, father. I was just thinking.'

'About what?' he enquired, and Jessie stopped what she was doing and regarded her daughter in the dim light of the crofthouse.

'Nothing much,' she answered evasively, ' Just stones on the beach.'

The other two exchanged a glance. They had noticed a change in the girl in the last day. She was fretful and looked concerned and they were worried that the fever might be working on her again. 'I'm going to check the creels in the boat this evening. I must go when the tide is low.'

Kirsten brightened. 'Oh Father, I would like to come with you.' Jessie cast a doubtful glance at her husband.

'Are you feeling up to coming with me?'

'Yes,' she answered emphatically.

'Well I suppose that will be all right. It should not take us too long. It is still as calm as a pond out there,' and he nodded towards the silence of the waveless sea that had been present all that day.

With a little objection from Jessie it was finally settled and the two would set off after their meal for the boat at Sanna. They rowed round behind the few small rocky islands that cluster in Sanna Bay, where Kirsten could see the long fronds of weed deep under the boat and shoals of small codling and pollach darting and feeding among it. They pulled up two of the creels and lifted out one large crab. Next they rowed the boat round the headland watching seals lying on the rocks warming themselves in the dying sun. An otter was sitting on a rock on the shore noisily tearing strips off a fish it was holding between its paws. The crunching grunting sound carried easily over the sea to the boat, and now seagulls began to circle over its head, hoping for scraps after it had moved off.

Everything was natural and peaceful. But tonight Kirsten had an uneasy feeling in the pit of her stomach and was desperate to get ashore. Jamie wanted to check his creels lying in the bay right at the foot of the Carraig Cliffs. The two of them rowed together, pulling the long oars and sending the small wooden boat along the coast, cutting the still water like a knife. Rowing this way they neared Kirsten's beach and she took her opportunity.

'Father, I am feeling very tired,' she said quite truthfully, for the restlessness of the previous night was beginning to catch up on her. 'Could you put me ashore at the bay.' She was pale, and tight lipped, such was the worry that engulfed her.

Jamie looked at her, unsure, and saw her drawn expression. He was still worried about her after the terrible week they had spent when she was missing. He considered for a moment and then answered, 'I suppose so. But I will still have to check the other creels.' Jamie took the oars and pulled, swinging the prow of the boat round and after a while onto the sandy shore. Kirsten scrambled out and gave the boat a push.

Her father pulled out again beyond the rocky headland and towards the Carraig Cliffs. She watched as his strong arms carried the boat into a small dot in the distance and then set about her task. The tide was now almost at its lowest ebb. Kirsten marked the rock, still under the water, near where she thought the stone had landed. It was about twenty feet from the shore, but she could probably wade out to it. The water was cold around her knees and as she walked she held her skirt high about her waist. The sand stirred under her feet and obscured her view. For ten minutes she waded back and forth with no success.

It was difficult to make anything out among the strands of freely swaying weed, but then her foot fell upon something hard and smooth. With a leap of expectation she curled her toes round it and succeeded in rolling it up the shin of her other leg to the surface, where she grabbed it before it could drop again to the bottom. She had it! In her hand lay a blue stone. Without doubt it was the Blue Orbed, glistening lightly in the dying light of the sun. It seemed an unremarkable stone and Kirsten could not for the life of her think why the stone men attached such importance to it.

Up until this point Kirsten had had no real notion or plan other than retrieving the stone. What was to happen next had not entered her head. Somehow she must take it to the caves, but her family would miss her if she did not arrive back long before Jamie. They would be worried and angry. But she must go through with this task. Hopefully she could pass the stone on to Choan, waiting at the cave mouth with his rope suspended from the high boulder and then bolt for freedom once more. If he was so eager to retrieve the stone in time for this night perhaps he would not pursue her. It was no more than delivering a message and going on her way. Yet in her heart Kirsten knew that it was not as simple as that.

Turning her face towards the cliffs she began her journey, keeping one eye on her father in his boat out on the water, rowing between the markers for his creels, and trying to keep out of his sight should he happen to look towards the shore. This made the going more difficult for her, for she had to work low on the skyline and behind as many of the large boulders and rocks as she could. Again and again she winced with pain as she stubbed her toes or bruised her knees and elbows on the rocks. With such slow progress the journey took her almost an hour.

The sun was set and the full moon was just beginning to rise, sending a shimmering, silver light across the water. Bats buzzed about her head, flying and swooping erratically, yet never colliding with anything. Out towards the islands a heavy bank of clouds was building up on the horizon. Ahead of them she was aware that the air was now chill and a stiff breeze was beginning to blow up causing white tops on the rising swell. There would be a gale before this night was out.

She looked towards Jamie in his boat. The rising breeze had been with him pushing him gently, unawares towards the cliffs. Only now had he become aware of it and it was clear to Kirsten watching on the shore that he was struggling to row against it. It might yet drive him past the headland, down the coast or out into the deep sea. Kirsten stood still, appalled. What should she do? She could not leave her father alone and in danger in the boat. Yet she still felt that she must complete this task; some other disaster would fall upon her, or all her people if she failed to return the stone to the stone men. Meanwhile her father was now flailing, helpless before the wind. She struggled long and hard with herself. This was the most difficult moment of her life. The choice was to run somehow to the aid of her father, whom she loved, or turn with the stone to the cave and Choan, for whom she felt almost nothing, but had an obligation, a duty to repay and a promise to fulfil.

She watched helplessly as Jamie struggled with the oars. He was turning the boat round to run with the wind. His only hope was to try and pull with it around the headland and try and run onto the shore further up the coast. Kirsten knew that most of that coast was rocky although there were sandy spits and beaches where he might just make a landfall. Miserably she realised that there was nothing she could do for Jamie, for by the time she had raised the alarm he would be out of sight, and as the gale rose, no one could go to his rescue. She must trust him to his own skill and good sense. She wanted to cry and to run for the comfort of her mother, but biting her lip she now turned her back on the sea and stumbled on with blurred, brimming eyes to the mouth of the great cave.

Here she stopped, hesitating, not wanting to go any further into the darkness of the cave and called out weakly, 'Choan.' There was silence. 'Choan!' Still nothing. 'Choan, are you there?' The only sound that reached her was that of the waves breaking on the rocks and the wind whistling through the crack. Cautiously Kirsten walked into the blackness of the cave. She groped along the wall, stumbling over the uneven, wet, muddy floor.

At length her hand fell upon the rough rope dangling loosely into the cave. She tugged it and called out for Choan again. There was no reply. What was she to do? It was hardly possible to leave the stone lying on the floor. It might just be feasible to tie it to the rope in the hope that Choan would pull it up later and find it. But every time she twisted the rope round it, the stone fell to the ground and she had to grope around in the dark to find it again. Eventually she realised that she would have to climb at least as far as the ledge, where she could more reasonably leave it to be found.

It was a difficult climb for the young girl. The rope swung wildly about in the air swinging her so that she crashed her knuckles and knees off the walls of the cleft as she worked her way up. Her arms ached and her hands were becoming chaffed on the rough twist of the cord. The climb seemed to go on for ever. Every movement of her arms and legs was worse than the last, till she feared that she would lose her grip and fall to the floor.

Eventually she completed her struggle to the edge of the ledge and heaved herself onto it panting. For a few minutes she lay there drawing her breath, listening to the wind howling past the entrance to the cave and to the rising roar of the waves on the rocks. How she hoped that Jamie had managed to pull himself ashore around the headland of the Carraig Cliff.

After a few minutes she pulled herself up to sitting position and leaning against the rocky wall felt around for a suitable place to leave the stone. The walls were mossy and cold, a damp sheen covered their surface. Her hand fell through a space in the rock face, wide and blank, the entrance to the tunnel that led on to the blue lochan. As she did so, a searing pain tore into her wrist, as suddenly an iron grip squeezed it so hard that she cried out in agony. A face thrust itself into hers, laughing cruelly, teeth bared in a grimace of pleasure, eyes bulging. 'Hagh!' cried a low growling voice, 'Hagh! We huv gott yow at lasst. The luttle prize is cum tow uss at lasst. Whot a luvly pressent now tow give tow the Mullach. Hagh! Hagh! Hagh! Oh he wull be pleased!'

Kirsten felt as if a bullock had kicked her in the stomach. Morlech? Morlech! She was caught like a rabbit in a trap.

Chapter 13

The Trial

As she stumbled along in front of Morlech with his heavy, stinking breath close on her, Kirsten cursed her stupidity. She should have left the stone on the beach and forgotten all about this awful place. She should have abandoned Choan to his fate, this was not her world after all. Why had she bothered to try and help him especially when her poor father was struggling on the sea? Gone was her chance to be of any use to him now. She was lost again as surely as a mouse torn from its nest by an eagle is lost forever. This time there would be no escape. Morlech meant her some evil mischief. He was shoving her on rapidly down the long passages and tunnels with great urgency. What was he about? Kirsten bit her lip in a mixture of frustration and fear.

'Hagh! Hagh! We have a luvly pressent for the Mullach. Will he nagt be pleased? Yess! Hagh! Hagh! Und this iss badd for Choan. Yess, yess! Verry badd! Hagh! Hagh!'

'Where is Choan, you beast!' shouted Kirsten at him. She was angry now, angry with herself and with Morlech. Bitterness filled her and with that a determination to be as troublesome to the horrible Morlech as she could be.

'Hagh! Hagh!,' laughed the stoneman growlingly. 'Yow will see. Yess! Hagh! Hagh!' He was lolling along with long strides, now half dragging Kirsten. 'Yess sune yow will see. Choan iss in great trubble und sune I wull have my revenge on him. Hagh!' He pulled her up a side tunnel that broke off from the main route that they were

112

following and through a narrow gap into a small dark cavern. Here were four men, whom Kirsten recognised as members of Morlech's clan.

'What have you done with Choan?' she persisted. 'Let me see him.'

He looked at her scornfully. 'No time now-times. We musst go. Hurrry, hurrry.' He was enjoying this small moment of triumph and obviously could not resist telling her of his pleasure. 'Choan iss a traitorr, trying tow lett yow go bak tow the high lands, tow warn yowr people abowt uss. We wude nagt be safe und the Mullach wull have the life of Choan forr that. Ut is jusst as well thut I cott yow befower yow wentt. I trackked huss root tow the great gate tow lett yow go. He hass escaped me again, butt only forr a luttle while. I know that he hass losst the Blue Orbed, though he nevverr deserved tow be its keeper ut all. Ut should have been owr famuly, nagt Choan's. Ut was owr right, nagt his. When the Mullach finds the stone gonne then Choan's fate wull be sure, Butt I amm gladd that we have yow as a proof tow the Mullach that Choan plans tow take on the Mullach und be the leader humself. Choan wull answer tow the Mullach now-times, for now-times is the Orbed-time, und yow, gurrl, are my proof that he is a hateful traitor tow the Mullach.'

Kirsten did not understand the threat, but realised that things were looking very black indeed, for her, for Choan and for Choan's clan, even if Morlech did not think she had ever been out of this underworld. She looked at the spiteful ire in Morlech's eyes and shuddered. He was pale in his victory. Now he turned to his comrades and said, 'We must go now-times, hurrry, hurrry.'

The party now marched along tunnels until they reached the steps that led downwards. Kirsten recognised them and knew that they would soon find themselves at the edge of the cavern of the blue lochan. When they did she was not struck with the awe and wonder she had experienced the first time she had seen it, following the bent form of old Crallogh. It is strange how after only a few days in this place, she had come to recognise many of its landmarks with the familiarity of home. Here was a curved marking on a rock and there a boulder that she had seen before on her frequent trips to the lochan with Choan's family. It was familiar and unsurprising.

All the time her mind was focusing on what might be about to happen, and how if at all, she would escape from this mess. She wanted to see Choan and tell him that she had the stone safe in a fold of her clothes but there was no sign of him – she was a prisoner. If only she could let him know that she had the stone, he might have some hope and she might yet win her freedom.

They jogged on through the meadow of moss and orchids. The soft moss cushioned her feet, springing gently under them as she moved. But there was no pleasure for her in the journey. Her hand strayed to the Kerala brooch, pinned to the front of her shawl where Sandy had replaced it as soon as she was well again and as she felt the sweep of the curved brass and the firmness of the blue stone in its centre, she thought of the beach, her beach where she was happy and secure – the beach where she had found this accursed stone. Would she ever see it again? Her hand tightened round the brooch and she heard Sandy's voice in her head, telling her of the perils he had endured on the seas. She saw his blue, peaceful eyes and heard his ready laugh. In the face of danger, he had always kept his head and taken it on. Strength filled her though she could not see how she would escape.

They were following the route to the dell where she had seen the Mullach. Again scattered groups of people were working their way across the sward towards it like starlings gathering on a tree. Kirsten had no idea what was going to happen that night, but she knew that her destiny was drawing on. Her heart was in her mouth as she walked.

Morlech took a swinging detour as they arrived near the hill which hid the dell from view. They skirted the base of it half darting and hiding behind tumbled rocks and boulders. He had the air of a man who was trying to move unseen, like a hunter – or the hunted, she could not tell which. At one point he pulled Kirsten violently into the lee of a great rock, until a group of men had walked on. In this fashion the small party approached the dell from the opposite side to the one from which Kirsten had entered it before. Deliberately Morlech moved his men around his captive so that she was hidden from the sight of anyone who might glance their way, and found a place behind a great rock where he hid Kirsten. His kinsmen stood erect. There was no way of escape.

Through a crack in the rock Kirsten could just see half of the cup of the dell. Her heart sank. There were thousands of stone men and women cramming the space – three, maybe four thousand – many, many more than she had seen the last time. Kirsten had not imagined so many could live in this strange world – and now they all sat silently, waiting. No one in the rest of the gathering place could see her, the captive of the grinning Morlech.

Soon Morlech's family came in and sat near the front of the assembly, grunting noisily and looking content with themselves. The dell was already almost full, but though she searched urgently for Choan and his clan she could find no sign of them. Then at last, reluctantly dragging their feet they entered the far side of the amphitheatre and shuffled uneasily into their places. All looked pale, unhappy and apprehensive. Choan was chalk-white, sweating and stood with his shoulders bent.

In a single glance Kirsten realised that he was in absolute despair. She wanted to leap up and cry out to him that she was safe and that she had the stone, but Morlech's ice like grip was tight around her wrist and she could not.

A dozen men climbed the rise to the dais and stood round the great stone slab in its centre. All of a sudden the silence was cracked as the voices of the assembly rose again into a chant just as they had done before. All the people were concentrating intently, chanting and staring at the dais, all that is except for the clan of Choan who hardly opened their mouths but kept glancing round with worried expressions, and Morlech who sat chuckling to himself. Kirsten looked at Morlech, his face contorted with evil pleasure, and shuddered. She must talk with Choan.

Then the Mullach entered the arena and all fell silent once more. With great ceremony the old man swung the Green Orbed off from around his neck and held it high above his head. It sparkled pale and jade in the half light of the cavern. Next he turned and signalled to Choan to approach. Kirsten watched with horrified wonder as Choan walked draggingly to the front, his arms limp by his sides, his eyes downcast.

'Whott iss the meening of thiss?' hissed the Mullach. 'Give me the Blue Orbed, Choan. Give ut me now-times'

'I… I… do nagt have ut,' stuttered Choan, trembling.

The Mullach drew himself up suddenly and shook with rage. 'Whott? Whott do yow mean? Nagt have ut? Yow do nagt have ut?'

'Oh Mullach,' began Choan, '…we have been keepers of the grate Blue Stone forr these lasst tenn generashuns. I do nagt know how ut came tow be losst butt ut hass been stolen fromm owr place.' Kirsten wanted to cry out, Choan looked so pale and terrified and she had the wretched stone on her. Again Morlech tightened his grip

116

around her and moistened his smiling lips. Choan continued, his voice trembling, 'Though I have looked everrry where I can nagt tell yow whho has taken utt or where ut is. Ut is losst… stolen,' and his eyes darted off in search of Morlech.

'How cann thiss be, Choan?' snapped the Mullach. 'Yow are the keeper, yow can nagt lett this be. Ut was entrusted to yowr care as ut has all times been with yowr folk. Neverr dud I thunk thatt yow could do such a thing. Where is ut? Tell me now-times. Tell me!' he finished with a shriek.

'I do nagt know. I do nagt know. I do nagt know,' answered the other dejectedly.

The crowd held its silence watching the old man glaring at Choan who stood stooped, hardly able to raise his eyes to look at the Mullach. Choan looked defeated and resigned to his fate.

'Ut woss the gurrl, Churstun, yow made uss keep, Oh Mullach.' The voice broke in on the hushed assembly like a thunderclap. All heads turned and saw Urick, Choan's son standing pale-faced and shaking in the midst of his family. His hands were on his hips and he faced the old man fiercely.

The Mullach looked at him with narrowing eyes. 'Exxsplain yowrself, Urick.'

'Ut woss the gurrl, Churstun,' he repeated. 'Yow ascked uss tow look afterr the gurrl fromm the high lands, und the stone can nagt be fownd sunce she came. She has been nuthing butt trubble sunce she came. She musst have ut.'

Beside him stood Crallogh. He nodded in agreement. 'Ut iss so,' and he looked pityingly at Choan. Kirsten pulled herself further into the shadow of the rock. What was she to do now? If they found the stone on her now then who would believe her story?

The Mullach looked back at Choan. 'Brung the gurrl

tow me!' he cried fiercely. 'I want tow see the gurrl. Hurry we have nagt mutch time.'

Choan looked even more dejected. 'I can nagt do thatt, Oh Mullach. I do nagt know where she iss.' Kirsten saw the shoulders of Morlech rise and fall as he struggled to suppress his mirth.

'I do nagt follow yow, Choan,' said the Mullach, very quietly. 'Yow do nagt know where she iss? Yow have losst her too?' Then his voice rose to shrieking crescendo, 'Have yow losst everythung – yowr famuly, yowr home, yowr boats,...yowr LIFE?' He jabbed his finger towards Choan and his eyes flared. Never had Kirsten seen such a menacing look. 'This iss verry, verry serious. Verrry, verry careless.' He thumped his hands together with a mighty crack and shouted, 'Yow wull answer forr this, Choan! Yow will answer wuth yowr life und the liffes of yowr chuldrun.'

A murmur spread through the assembled crowd. The Mullach turned and swept his hand in the air over them and as he did so the Green Orbed sparkled casting darting, green rays around the cavern. 'Neverr have we had an Orbed-time without the Blue Stone. I can nagt say now whether the time has cumm forr us tow return tow owr lands for without ut, the great warriurr can nagt speak. I need the Blue Orbed und great wull be the reward und the honour given tow the famuly that brungs me the gurrl orr the Blue Stone, now-times.'

This was the moment that Morlech had been waiting for. He leapt to his feet and cried out in a loud voice, 'Oh Mullach, I have the present forr yow, the sweet tenderr morsell that yow wull want.' With that he hauled Kirsten out from her place. A gasp rose from the company, Choan quivered and shook where he stood, a look of bewilderment and disbelief on his face.

'Brung her down tow me,' snapped the Mullach.

Kirsten was quickly thrust forwards by Morlech who

grabbed her harshly by the arm and marched her down to the foot of the dais. She looked straight at the Mullach and saw in his face a mixture of interest, anger and confusion. For a moment he did not speak, but then quietly and menacingly he asked, 'Well then, gurrl, where have yow hiddenn the blue stone? Yow will answer tow me. Uf yow arr fownd to have ut yow wull die, gurrl. I sware ut by the Green Orbed, yow wull die!... Und,' he added in a hoarse, low voice, 'Choan und his kin wull be spayred.'

She was trapped. Kirsten did not know what to say. 'The... the ston... stone?' she stalled.

But the Mullach saw more in her eyes than she could hide from him. 'Yow know abowt the stone. Yow have the stone, or yow know att least wherre ut is. Is that nagt so?' He almost whispered. Kirsten was casting around wildly in her mind for some way to explain the stone hidden in her shawl. She could not be found with it now. 'Where have yow been gurrl? Yow have been mussing, have yow nagt?'

Morlech broke in excitedly, 'Yuss! Yuss! I fownd her trying tow escape from the great gate, before I captured her tow bring her here. She was almost away owt to the high lands.'

'I was not trying to escape!' cried out Kirsten indignantly. She smarted at the memory of Morlech's bitter grip on her arm. How dare he tell such a lie! How dare he! Yet she could not work out what to answer without incriminating herself.

'Why werre yow at the great gate thenn?' quizzed the Mullach, 'if yow were nagt trying tow escape. Yow musst have had a reason. Yow have been mussing, und yow were captured there is ut nagt so?'

'I... I... I was trying to find Choan,' said the girl with perfect truth.

'Why?'

119

'I was just looking for him.'

'Yow were trying tow escape und I caught yow, yow liar. Yow were neerly away und yow would have been if I had nagt caught yow. Yow crawling, sneeking, wurthless wurrm.' Morlech spat and grunted as he spoke and looked sideways at the Mullach to see how he was reacting to this small triumph. He was acting his part well.

Kirsten was thinking quickly now. Was Morlech playing a game, or did he really not know that she had been out on the high lands?

'Morlech have yow got the stone as well?' asked the Mullach turning from Kirsten.

'Nagt, master! Thatt I do nagt have.' He looked uncertain and, for a moment, evasive. With a sudden flash of insight Kirsten realised that Morlech did not know where the stone was. Perhaps he still believed that it was lost or that Choan might yet produce it and Kirsten realised that for some reason he did not think or believe that she had anything to do with the stone.

'Ah, Morlech, I thought that yow would have brott me thatt prize as well,' said the Mullach reproachfully. 'The time of the Orbed is allmosst uponn us. Tow be surre of the message we need the blue stone.' He spoke with urgency and now raised his head and looked slowly over the crowd in the amphitheatre. 'Again I say tow you all. If enny mannn knows where the Blue Orbed is then great shall be his rewarrd. I sware upon the green stone (und this is a binding oath thut cann *neverr* be brokenn) thut they wull have enything they want, thut I have the powerr tow give. Und so ut wull be for enny who cann tell me who ut was thut took the stone. By the green stone I swear thatt they shall have enything they ask. Butt thatt person, who took the stone, shall die, und all his close-famuly,wife, sons und dotters.'

Kirsten was thinking furiously now. What chance did

she have if she was found here with the stone? None! They would simply assume she had stolen it and that would be that. The Mullach was intent on killing not just the one who had stolen the stone, but their family as well. But who was it who had taken it? She had not the faintest idea. Even if she had, could she prove it? Everything seemed stacked against her, everything pointed to her guilt, even though she was completely innocent. Somehow she must try and fix the blame where it belonged. If she could do that then might she not yet ask the Mullach for what she wanted – her freedom – for had he not made that promise on the green stone? His oath was binding – '… they will have anything they want that I have the power to give.' He would have to do it. There might yet then be a chance if only she could work out how the stone had managed to find itself on the beach.

Absolute stillness descended on the gathering and the Mullach cast his penetrating eyes slowly over every soul in the amphitheatre. As he looked the others gazed back until their eyes fell and looked away from his piercing stare. He was searching for any hint of untruth about them, any hint that they might be responsible. Kirsten too looked around. She looked at Morlech a sneer curling his lip horribly.

The Mullach's eye fell upon Crallogh and he saw him shift uneasily under his gaze. Kirsten saw it as well. Did Crallogh know something? Was *he* somehow responsible for the missing stone? He would have had plenty of opportunity to steal it and he had complained to Choan about his judgement. He always seemed dissatisfied with Choan's leadership. But why would he do such a thing? Did he want to be leader of Choan's clan instead, or was he just uneasy because he knew the truth of Kirsten's disappearance?

The Mullach moved on. Choan held his gaze well. He knew that letting Kirsten go had been wrong and he knew the danger he was in, but he was honest and was hiding nothing behind his deep, slatey gaze.

It was in that next moment that something caught Kirsten's eye, something she could not believe. It was a glimpse of something so out of place in that dark world that it hit her with the force of a bolt of lightning, and as she saw it the veil was suddenly lifted and she understood.

Urick shifted uneasily. The Mullach was about to look in his direction and Choan was pale and placed a protective hand on his shoulder as he looked at his son.

Kirsten leapt forward and with a sudden cry called out, 'I...I was looking for Choan...I was looking for Choan, be...be...because I wanted to give him this!' With a flourish she drew out the blue stone from under her shawl and held it above her head. 'I found it and I wanted to give it to him, the keeper of the blue stone.'

All eyes now turned and looked at her, the Mullach glowered, and Morlech's eyes widened in consternation and amazement. It was he who spoke first, crying out with joy, 'See! See, Hagh! Hagh! Her guilt iss before yow. See! she hass the stone afterr all. I knew she had hidden ut. She has ut, she is gillty. I jusst wanted tow prove tow yow that she had ut. I caught herr trying tow steal ut und take ut away tow the high lands where ut would be losst forever. I brought the gurrl tow yow, Oh Mullach und I brought the blue stone tow yow. Hagh! Hagh! I dudd ut.'

The Mullach turned on Kirsten fiercely. 'What say yow, gurrl? Why have yow gott the stone? Speak, for yowr possession of ut speaks of yowr guilt.'

Kirsten knew now who had taken it but she spoke slowly and quietly. 'I found it in the ground, and I brought it back because I am part of Choan's clan.'

'Who took ut then?' demanded the Mullach sarcastically.

Kirsten hesitated. Perhaps she could save her skin if

she spoke up. One word, that was all that was required, the name of the one she knew had taken the stone. If she spoke the Mullach would have to honour his oath, she could be free. She looked at Choan pale and trembling and remained silent.

'Speak upp! If yow can tell me then I will spare yowr life,' cried the Mullach. 'If nagt, then we shall know thatt yow have guilt right enough und yow now know the punnishmentt for taking the stone.' Still Kirsten said nothing. 'Speakk!!' he shrieked, but Kirsten did not speak. She uttered not a word. She could not.

A pale shaft of light broke into the space from somewhere high up on the roof of the cavern. The Mullach spat fiercely on the ground and grabbed the stone from Kirsten's hand, turned and hurried up to the dais. 'Bind herr!' he cried, 'We wull deal with her after-times for the time of the Orbed has arrived.'

Two men grabbed Kirsten roughly and bound her with cords. Then all the assembly arose and faced the dais. The Mullach took first the green stone and set it over a notch marked in the very centre of the stone table in the middle of the dais. He then rushed over to the huge carving on the stone wall of the cave and clambering over the face of the rock with an agility that defied his age, set the blue stone in a cavity cut to be the eye of that huge, carved form of a man

The Mullach scrambled back down to the ground, turned and looked up. Following his gaze, Kirsten saw for the first time that high up on the roof of the cavern, which was a hundred feet or more above their heads, there was a small hole. Through this a faint pale light filtered, and as they watched the light grew in intensity, a silver, white light. The ray of the light grew and spread and Kirsten realised that it was a shaft of moonlight, breaking in from her world to this place. The full moon must be swinging over the very cleft that ran down through the rocks to the spot on the dais. Ever brighter the beam became until it cast a piercing white light right onto the centre of the dais, so bright in the gloom of the cavern that it almost hurt Kirsten's eyes. In that radiance the green stone seemed to come to life.

A sudden halo of dancing green light shone from the Green Orbed, as if the stars themselves were dancing before her eyes. This light reflected in turn off the roof of the cavern whose walls became alive with sparkling, scintillating points of diamond white light. Then (as the moon rolled past the opening high above) the angle of the light shifted, suddenly focusing into a beam and fell upon a point on the wall of the cavern. The outline of the man carved on the rock was clearer now. Kirsten could see clear stones set in his forehead, his breast and on each hand. The reflected light fell upon these so that they glowed dimly, sparkling very faintly like far distant stars. And then it focused upon the Blue Orbed set in the cavity of the man's eye. Suddenly the blue stone shone strongly and it was as if all the intensity of the moonbeam was channelled into it. A piercing blue light spread all around and all over the assembled people. A growling sound rose from the people in the dell.

'The eye of the Pixts is shining, at lasst' cried the Mullach 'At lasst the time has cumm forr us tow returrn tow the high lands und take back our place. The eye of the Pixts has spokenn.' A great cheer rose from the crowd, a chilling sound like the rumble of a volcano and all the men and women rose to their feet and beat their hands on their breasts. 'Now yow musst return tow yowr homes, my people und gett yowrselves reddy. For at the now-times ut is rite forr us tow return tow the high lands. They are owrs!'

The Mullach turned now to Kirsten. 'As for yow, yow are nagt of this people. Yow stole the stone. Yow musst die, butt not now-times, nagt at the Orbed-time, for ut is beauiful und precious time. Und we have wurk tow do. Yow I give unto the care of Morlech, untill I call forr yow.'

Morlech turned and looked at the Mullach with great expectation of honour for recovering the stone and Kirsten, 'Yow will keep herr safe,' said the Mullach. 'For now-times I believe Choan that he does nagt know how the stone was losst. Take the gurrl und see that she does nagt escape, Morlech.'

Morlech spat in disgust, but obeyed.

Chapter 14

Release

Kirsten sat miserably in the dark recess of a small cave, trying to understand what was happening. For thousands of years the Blue Orbed had never shone. But now this lost race thought they had received a message from it. Why it should have happened the day Kirsten had brought the stone back and not on any of the similar Orbed days over these thousands of years, she could not know. Perhaps in his hurry the Mullach put the stone in the wrong spot. If she had never brought the Orbed back, then they would never have thought the time was right to return to the high lands – her land. Now they were going to try and take back *her* land and it was all her fault. They would come on her family unawares and kill them. If only she had not brought the stone back...

A sound outside the stone door of her cell roused Kirsten from these dark thoughts. What was it? A sigh – a light breath? It came again. Very soft words, hardly spoken above a whisper reached her. She could not make them out. Very slowly and cautiously the door of her prison was silently rolled back, inch by inch until a crack just wide enough for her to squeeze through was revealed.

'Cumm onnn!' hissed a voice very quietly, 'Cumm, cumm!'

Kirsten eased herself through the gap and found herself standing again in the small passage. In front of her was a hunched dark form.

'Urick!' she began to cry, but quickly the boy clapped

126

his hand over her mouth and both waited silently. No noise stirred from the adjacent chamber. 'Stull asleep,' he whispered, 'They are resting for the great battull. Cumm follow, butt be verry quiet. Dow yow hear?'

Kirsten was perplexed, but obeyed as Urick limped off ahead of her, dragging his weak leg behind him. He would not let her speak for a long time, but led her through a series of twisted tunnels and tracks away from her prison. They squeezed through many gaps and tunnels until they were sitting on a ledge high up in the cavern of the blue lochan. From this point Kirsten could see the whole of the great arena, the dwellings, the animals and the constant, glittering glow of the water. Now she could see crowds of stone men gathering on the plain before her. Thousands of them, and all of them were carrying heavy mattocks and cudgels – they were armed for battle. Kirsten's mouth went dry. At last Urick turned to her and spoke.

'Yow musst cumm with me und gett tow the great gate tow go back tow the high lands. Now-times.'

'But why, Urick?' gasped the girl amazed.

'Yow musst be allowed tow go free und take yowr chance,' he answered.

Kirsten still did not understand, 'You mean that Urick? Free? But what about all this?'

Urick looked at the army gathering below her. 'Yess, yess they are cumming. Cumming tow take back the high lands. Worriurs fromm oll cornurs of owr land. But, Churstun, yow see...if it were nagt forr yow, my father would be dead und...' he hesitated looking away from her, '...I too. Yow saved his life und my life und yow musst olso have the chansse. Forr, yow see,' and again he hesitated, 'I took the stone.' Urick hung his head as he spoke and did not look at Kirsten.

'I know,' said Kirsten softly, 'I saw your footprints on the beach, Urick.' He looked at her amazed and she

127

continued, 'It was only when I saw you with the spyglass…'

'Whott?' he broke in.

She pointed to a bulge in the wrap he was wearing around his shoulder, and reaching over, drew out Hughie's spyglass. 'I saw it when the Mullach was about to look at you, under the fold of your cloth. That is a precious thing that belongs to my brother. You found it on the rocks the night you lost the Orbed, Urick. Didn't you?'

'Yuss,' he sighed dejectedly, 'Thiss looked so speshull. Butt how dud yow know that I was there?'

'The footprints I saw on the beach were of a man. limping. It had to be you. But why did you take the Orbed, Urick? I don't understand.'

He looked straight at her now for the first time. 'I saw Morlech creeepping arround the place where owr famuly keep owr preshus things. I knew the Orbed was there und thatt when we went up tow the high lands for the animuls thatt he mightt take the Orbed. So I took ut with me that night. Ut was only when we gott back tow owr home that I realised thatt ut was gonn. I spent all my time fromm then trying tow find ut. Butt always Morlech was creeping abowt looking, searching forr ut. He didd nagt really know that ut was losst. He thought that Choan musst have hiddenn ut until the day thatt my father told himm ut was misssing. Yow, Churstun, saved my father's life by findung the stone and mine by nagt telling thut I had taken ut. Why didd yow nagt tell them?' He looked at her curiously.

'There was no other way,' she said, 'It was my life or yours, you see.'

Urick remained silent for a moment looking at her, in wonder, then suddenly he spoke, 'Cumm now und we shall gett yow free.'

'Yes! Yes!' cried the girl, then hesitating added, 'Urick

what will they do when the find I'm gone? Will they not take you and kill you anyway?'

'They wull nagt find me owt,' he said confidently, I cann cuvver my trackxs. Butt iff they do – thenn my father und my famuly wull be safe anyhowe. Und yow, yow cann take yowr famuly away safe beforre owr people cumm tow the high lands.' Kirsten looked at him in amazement. She had disliked Urick from the moment that she had first seen him, and yet here he was now ready to risk his own life for her.

He pulled her up to her feet and hissed again in a low whisper, 'Thiss way.'

Urick led on through the tunnels often pausing and listening silently for any hint of sound. Once or twice he bade Kirsten wait alone in the dark recesses of some space while he went on ahead to reconnoitre, returning to indicate that they dart off in another direction. So they toiled and after perhaps an hour they reached the steps that led to the level of the great gate. A fierce wind blew in through the tunnel and down the walls of the cave water was pouring in torrents. Until then, Kirsten had forgotten the storm that was brewing when she had fallen back into this deadly world a few hours before. Now she remembered with despair her poor father struggling with his boat in the face of the rising gale. Had he managed to beach his boat on the shore?

They were now a hundred yards short of the entrance and lightning was flashing outside, sending the crouching form of Urick into a giant shadow on the walls and roof of the cave. After such a long dry spell, the water was finding new and easy courses down through the mud and loose scree of the hillside into this hidden cavern. At that moment, as Kirsten caught the sound of the waves crashing on the shore, there came an almighty crack, followed by a thunderous rumble. Whether the stone of the cave itself had been hit by lightning or the pouring waters had loosened rocks upon the hillside, Kirsten could not tell. But all of a sudden her ears were filled with the deafening roar of rocks falling around her, and the smell of mud.

The two crouched against the wall until the roar had ceased. Cautiously Urick raised himself up and proceeded with Kirsten crawling at his heels. He turned to her despair once more in his eyes. 'Ut is no use, Churstun, the way is blockked. Blockked forr everr.'

Kirsten looked at him disbelievingly. 'No!' she cried. 'It cannot be. No! No!' She shoved past him and crawled along the passage where loose bits of scree still teetered and fell dangerously around her. A faint light from outside was just visible, falling on the walls and crazy jumble of rocks. Stretching forward she thrust her hand through a gap under a great rock that had fallen and could feel the cool air and the wind whistle in. They could only be a few yards from the ledge at the great gate, and yet they could never hope to pass it, for barring their way was a huge slab of rock and hundreds of men could not have budged it if they tried. The path was blocked and Urick was right, it would be blocked for ever. Kirsten was ready to weep.

She looked at Urick. He was shaking, his brow was wet and he was wringing his hands. For a few minutes he did not speak. The situation was utterly hopeless. Then he turned and faced her. 'Cumm, Churstun. There is anuther way... only ut is verry dangerous. Dow yow want tow try ut?'

She nodded weakly. Anything to be free. What could be more dangerous than this? Urick picked his way carefully through the debris of the rock-fall and gingerly worked again through the tunnels. They doubled back down the steps until suddenly both were brought up short by the sound of a great drumming emanating from the ground under them. Urick paled. 'They have fownd that yow are mussing,' he said. 'We have nagt gott much time.'

Now Urick ran as best he could dragging his lame leg behind him. Often he halted, pulling Kirsten into crevices or recesses, and twice the two crouched motionless as the padded feet of stone men ran past their hiding spot. They were close to the great cavern and the people were searching for Kirsten as they made their preparations for the great battle. Urick led on. Kirsten followed, unsure where she was. Her lungs burned with the effort of crawling and running. Always Urick halted her if he sensed or heard anyone coming. At one point they turned a corner and saw a few paces off the rear of a form that even Kirsten recognised at a glance and her heart stood still. It was Morlech. He stopped and cocked his head like a dog to listen. Urick and Kirsten were completely without a place to hide. The rock here had no crevices or cracks. They stood as still as deer on a hill, holding their breaths until Kirsten thought that she would burst, her heart hammering in her breast.

After an age he moved off without turning and very cautiously the two followed. The further they travelled the busier the route seemed to become. By some curious instinct Urick seemed to know when to stop and when to dart into some space to conceal themselves. They crawled on their bellies again and again and squeezed through impossible gaps that a grown man would have failed to cross. Kirsten ached all over and almost wished that she would be captured again and put out of her misery.

Gradually she became aware of the sound of falling water and as they drew nearer, the din rose to a tremendous cascade. There was the smell of the sea in her nostrils and the taste of salt upon her lips. They entered a space where Kirsten saw a waterfall plummeting from a narrow cleft high in the roof of the cave to a chasm that went on and on into the blackness of the heart of the earth. It must have been hundreds of feet deep for the mist of the fall was lost far into the inky depths of the hole.

'Thiss,' said Urick, ' iss the well of the solt watterr. Ut is narrow und no one ever thinks there us a way owt to the high lands. Butt there is. My father's father's father wunce hud tow go this way tow the high lands. No wun hass everr dunn ut sunce-times, or before-times.'

Kirsten looked at the wet, slippery and almost sheer rock face and the force of the water cascading down its walls in disbelief. How could she manage that? It was a difficult climb for the most able bodied man but for her it was surely impossible. Yet what was her choice? Death or imprisonment forever, here in the world of the stone men or death by falling from the great height of this cave? Perhaps there was a minute chance of freedom if she followed Urick's way. She nodded weakly again to Urick. 'Yes I'll try it,' she said. The words came thickly and huskily from her lips.

He looked at her with admiration. 'I shall climb summ way,' he said, 'forr I have dunn summ of the way before-times.'

'What will they do with you when they find out that you have helped me, Urick?' asked Kirsten.

He shrugged and said, 'I wull say that yow musst have escaped beforre the great rock fell at the great gate. My father wull say thut I wass wuth the famuly, forr I amm sure that he really thunks thut thut iss where I amm.'

Before she turned to set off Kirsten looked hard at Urick. This would be the end of her meeting with the stone men. If she succeeded in the climb she would be free. If she failed, what did it matter any more? 'Thanks, Urick.' she said, then with a sudden movement unclipped the Kerala Brooch from her shawl and gave it to the boy. 'Keep this,' she said and say that you found it by the great gate. And...' she added hesitantly, 'remember me by it. It is for you.'

Urick looked at her and then slowly drew the spyglass from his clothing. 'Yowrs,' he said.

Kirsten took it and stuffed it into her shawl. 'Let us go then.'

The climb was hard and painful. The rock was slippery and had Urick not been behind her Kirsten would certainly have fallen several times. He gripped her feet and directed her hands onto footholds on the rock face so that they made their way slowly and painstakingly up the surface. Eventually the holds became easier, a series of ledges and clefts, so that it was more like climbing a ladder or a stair than a rock face. Around them the roar of the falling water was deafening. Kirsten looked up and saw that the only way on was to plunge into the very cleft through which the water surged and fell, forming the waterfall itself. She looked back hopelessly at Urick.

'There's no way on.'

He nodded vigorously and shouted to her above the roar, 'Ut is right, Churstun, ut is the way.'

'But there is no way.'

'My father's father's father, saidd, ut was nott farr, butt yow havve tow climb fasst.'

Kirsten looked doubtfully at the crevice again, at the fall beneath her and at the eyes of Urick. She wavered and was ready to give up. Then a movement caught her eye. Sliding and slipping on the rock face some distance below the two of them was the scrambling form of a single climber. It turned its face upwards and Kirsten had a full view of the bared, yellow teeth and grimacing face of Morlech. He climbed with great speed and skill and would soon be level with them. Urick followed her gaze. 'Go onn, Churstun, go onn! Leave Morlech tow me. Hurrry, hurrry.'

'Alright,' she said hesitating, 'and thanks, Urick.'

For a brief moment the two looked at each other. Each from a very different world. Two worlds unable to live together. Two peoples who longed for the land of Kirsten's home. Understanding bound them in that moment, the understanding of shared dreams and the need for a home and family. Then Kirsten turned without another word and began climbing.

Urick was right – the handholds were now easy and she made good progress. But soon the pressure of the water was forcing down on her head and shoulders, the cold icy water of the sea. Her hands ached with cold and gripping the rock and she thought that she would never be able to force herself up against the power of the water. Below her she caught angry shouts and cries and glancing down saw Morlech and Urick struggling with each other on a ledge. Each was trying to force the other over. From below came the voice of Urick carried faintly against the din, 'Go onn Churstun. Go onn!' Above her the water issued through a gap little wider than two men. This, according to Urick was the final exit and it seemed impossible. She could see light through the gap, a dim, shimmering light, like the surface of water seen from below, flowing in through the funnel of the cleft like a pale green moonlight. It seemed there was only yards to go to reach the surface.

She took a deep breath and plunged into the gap and as she did so she heard a horrified cry from below as of a voice falling, fading into the depths of the great chasm. Kirsten dared not look back and see whether Urick, or Morlech, or both had plummeted from that precarious ledge. She pushed on with all her strength as the water filled her nose and ears. The force of the water was almost too much for her, driving her back down and into the cavern beneath, but with a final, mighty effort she thrust on and suddenly found the water quieter as she passed through the gap and into the swirling waters above. She was flailing and twisting in the water, now and struck out instinctively, swimming upwards, chest burning as she ran out of breath until finally, her head broke the surface and she found herself free to gasp. Around her the water was wild, tossing still in the teeth of a gale. It was daylight, pale and grey with rain whipping around her ears and the swell rising and falling all around her like mountains. She had made it, she was free – but what freedom? She had been cast out into the middle of a raging sea.

Chapter 15

Reprieve

Kirsten was a good swimmer but she had never swum in a stormy sea before, nor heavily laden with sodden clothes. It was bitterly cold and as she struggled to keep afloat she regained her breath in painful gasps. It seemed to her that she must have been cast out somewhere in the middle of the ocean, for all she could see was the sea around her, and she cursed Urick. She had believed him, trusted him, all he had done was kill her as surely as if he had pushed her from a great height. He had never been through the gap, so how did he know where it would throw her up? What a bitter end – drowning at sea! Had he given his life as well for her to end like this?

Then she twisted round and saw to her relief, not a hundred yards behind her, a rocky shore line. She had come to the surface gazing out to sea and had thought there was no land near her, but now she realised that the hole must have been close to the land after all.

Arms flailing in the icy water, she began to struggle towards the shore. Several times her head fell beneath the waves and she laboured to get back to the surface. Then, when she had almost given up hope her hand fell upon something hard floating on the water. Wood! Grabbing it she used it as a float, and kicking her legs made for the shore. At first, as she clung on desperately, she did not realise what it was, but then she suddenly recognised it. An oar! An oar from her father's boat!

Kirsten's purpose and hope had almost faded but this discovery gave her a final spur and she worked again against the waves towards the land. At last she felt the rocks beneath her feet and with great difficulty pulled herself clear of the falling swell after a great wave threw her violently onto the rocks. She slumped exhausted and panted for several minutes until she regained enough breath to drag herself out of the waves.

Only then did she lift her head and look around to take her bearings. The coastline had been unfamiliar while she had been in the sea. For all she knew she might have walked right under the sea to one of the islands, Muck or Eigg, or under Ardnamurchan itself to Mull. Now she recognised the headland and with relief realised that she had arrived further along her familiar coast round the headland of the Carraig Cliffs by only a few miles.

Grey light was now filling the sky and with it some of the force of the storm was waning. A few hundred yards off, along the rocky shore, she caught sight of a brown object and, with a cry, thought she recognised it. Kirsten scrambled over the rocks as fast as her weary limbs could take her until she could be sure and then approached it quickly but with trepidation. It was her father's boat. Lying beside it lay Jamie, cold and pale faced, unmoving. Kirsten cried out in despair and fell to her knees beside him.

'Father! Father!' she cried, 'I'm sorry,' and she hugged him to her. I am too late, was all she could think.

But then the man gave out a low moan.

'Kirsten…Kirsten? Is that you?'

Relief filled her. He was still alive. 'Yes father! Oh yes. I saw you struggling in the storm.'

Now that he had been found Jamie roused himself. He was bitterly cold, exposed on the rocks all night. 'My leg, Kirsten,' he croaked. Kirsten looked down and saw his leg twisted awkwardly under him. It was broken. What was she to do? The tide was still on the rise and with the full moon forcing it up the shore the rocks where they were sitting would soon be under water. The cliff behind them meant that they were effectively trapped and with Jamie's leg broken she could not move him. Their only hope lay in the boat, but although the wind was easing slightly it would still be exceedingly difficult and dangerous to move along the shore. There was, however, no other option.

Pushing the battered boat into the water she secured it in the lee of a rock where a large tidal pool acted like a small lochan. Painfully Jamie shunted himself into the bottom and lay as still as he could. Kirsten found the two oars and once the tide had risen far enough, pushed the boat out of their pool and into the swell of the sea. The wind had now swung round from the north which had the effect of helping push the small boat out from the rocks. For an hour, exhausted, Kirsten rowed and rowed and never seemed to make any headway. Jamie swooned in pain and frustration and lay in the bottom of the boat praying. It seemed again that they would eventually be thrust once more onto the jagged rocks and be wrecked, and Kirsten slumped over the oars in despair.

It was at that moment that the two heard a hail drifting over the wind. 'Jamie...! Kirsten...!' Kirsten looked round and saw to her disbelief, a larger boat coming in through the treacherous rocks. Its sail was set, six men were at the oars and at the helm, giving the orders stood Sandy, his seaman's eyes piercing the surface of the water and reading every hidden hazard under it. After an age he finally manoeuvred the larger boat along side and secured a tow rope.

'Jamie, Kirsten,' he cried, 'we thought we had lost you in the gale. We had given up all hope for you.'

'It was Kirsten,' croaked Jamie painfully from the bottom of the boat, 'she managed to save us from the rocks.'

Sandy looked at her with wonder, but said nothing.

Setting his sails, he turned the boat around and headed for home.

In Plocaig that night there was once more great rejoicing. Against all hope Jamie and Kirsten had been found alive, for no one had thought that they could ride out the storm and presumed they would have been driven far out into the sea and lost for ever. Only when the storm had died enough had Sandy felt it safe to take the other boat out to search for them.

'Ah but you two do not know how lucky you are to be alive,' observed Sandy. 'I have seen boats go down in lighter weather than that. I thought we had lost you for ever.'

Jessie gave out a cry as she bathed the wound on her husband's broken and now splinted leg. 'Don't be saying such a thing, Sandy,' she said, 'They are home.'

In a corner of the room lying on a small stool sat the spyglass. Hughie was looking at it thoughtfully. 'Aye and that is not all that's found,' he said. 'Imagine that floating down to near where you were, Kirsten. Sandy, it is a fine piece is it not? A cork case to allow it to float. A great gift from you. I always loved it and was furious with Kirsten when she lost it.'

'A fine gift indeed!' exclaimed Sandy, 'but the best gift is to have these two home safe, is it not?' Hughie grunted his agreement before Sandy continued, 'I remember the day I bought it from a man who makes telescopes and instruments in Bilbao. You won't find a better one this side of the Equator.'

Kirsten looked at Sandy standing by the fire warming his hands and swaying with the gentle rocking motion he had, as if he were forever on the bridge of his ship. 'Uncle Sandy,' she said, quietly, 'I'm sorry.'

'For what, Kirsten?' he answered puzzled.

'I haven't the brooch any more.' He looked at her with a surprised look.

'Never mind,' he said at last, 'I would rather you lost the brooch than that we lost you.'

Kirsten sat and stared silently into the heart of the burning fire. The flames licked the edge of the peat,s curling upwards with hissing smoke. Outside the wind whistled round the thatch and it brought back to her the howling cries of the stone men.

For the first time since her adventures had begun, she felt safe. The way for the great army of the stone men to come back was blocked. They could never pass again in to the high lands. They were locked in their caverns and passages, where they had lived for thousands of years and no doubt would live for thousands more. She thought how close they had all come to being faced with the terrors of that other world humming beneath their feet, a world now separated from them for ever, and she thought with a shudder how nearly she had been trapped too. Only she knew how close she had been to being lost forever, lost from the familiar sounds of the birds, the peewits, the gulls, the roar of the ocean, the blowing of the wind, the smell of the peat and the bog myrtle, the sound of the otters on the shore and the deer on the hills, the sight of the sun sinking red and burning from a crimson sky into the calm ocean; and lost from the warmth and love of her family and home. No one else need ever know.

Only one thought troubled her. What of Urick? He had risked his life so that she might be free. Had that been his death cry she heard as he fell, or was it Morlech? She would never know.

Afterwards

This was the tale that Kirsten told me so many years ago, the story that I had dismissed as a fable and rejected outright. It would have remained lost to me (and the world) had I not been forced, by my conscience, to explore it after certain curious events occurred.

Last summer was the wettest ever recorded in the west of Scotland. From March through to mid-August it rained on every day, not half hearted, smirry west-highland rain, but constant heavy downpours, like a tropical monsoon. It raised the level of the lochs and the burns to a point that washed away the banks of old pools and soaked the bogs so thoroughly that sheep were lost in the wet mud of their deepest reaches. New streams formed on the hillsides and there was an early run of salmon and trout into the lochs because the waters were so high.

I was out fishing by myself for mackerel, in my boat, near the Carraig Cliffs, but had had little luck. It was about time to give up and head for home when my rod suddenly arched and I reeled in hard. It was not a great fish but still it fought with vigour until at last it broke the surface at the edge of the boat. What met my eyes was the strangest looking fish I had ever seen. Huge black eyes like saucers on an oversized head, a gaping mouth, three large spikes on its back and the brightest imaginable colour of yellow on its belly.

At first I thought it a goby or a sea scorpion, both plentiful in those parts, but it was so very different. I had never seen anything like it and thrust my net into the water underneath it to land it. At that moment the fish gave a great twist and thrashed, tearing itself free from my hook and swam back deep into the sea and out of sight. I had no idea what this fish could be and spent the next weeks scouring the fishing books for any description, or picture, of a similar creature. There was none.

Only then, like a call from a far hilltop, did a vague memory of the fish in Kirsten's tale come back to me. I resisted, but eventually the idea grew on me. Was it possible that, with the flooding of the land, some route for such a creature to escape from the blue lochan had emerged? I confess that for some days I fished the same spot in the hope of catching another of the yellow bellied creatures, but with no success.

A few weeks later I was walking in the hills between the now deserted villages of Plocaig and Glendrian. They lie now in tumbled ruins. At the head of a small glen I came across a small stony outcrop. As I stood I heard what I took to be the sound of humming as wind blew through a gap in the stones. It was a rhythmic beating noise, a faint wisp of a sound and as soon as I heard it, it seemed to fade into the air. For an hour I scoured the rocks but could make nothing of it. Was this the spot where Sandy had heard the strange humming too?

By now the flesh of Kirsten's tale was coming back to me and my imagination was running riot. Early September had arrived and a late spell of warm and calm weather had finally arrived. One day I walked round to the Carraig Cliffs and picnicked on the shingle beach at their foot. The view over the islands was crystal clear and spectacular. I imagined Kirsten sitting on her own beach just along the coast and looking at the same scene, years before pondering the footprints on the shore. Then I plunged into the blackness of the great cave.

It is a very difficult climb from the floor of the cave to the great boulder lodged sixty feet up in the great cleft, but with ropes and the tools of a modern climber I managed it in half an hour. Beyond the great boulder and hidden from sight, I found a wide ledge. By now my heart was pounding in anticipation. Issuing from the ledge was an opening about the height and width of two men, but it was blocked by several huge fallen rocks. At the bottom was a crack into which I thrust my arm. Beyond these rocks, a great space seemed to open out.

As I withdrew my arm, my hand fell upon a small hard object, cold, wet and covered in moss and mud. I had no idea what it might be, but the feel of it intrigued me and I thrust it into a pocket, to examine later. At last, before descending I flashed the torch beam into the gap and squinted into the space beyond. The passage clearly did open out into a wider space again, but soon it curved out of sight beyond another fall of massive rocks. How far it went it was impossible to say, but the floor was smooth where it was free of fallen debris, I fancied it looked like a path.

It was only later, when I had returned home, that I took the object out and examined it properly. At first it seemed no more than a curiously shaped stone covered in the mud and debris of a bat ridden cave. It took an hour or more to clean it up and as I did so I sat in wonder. Now as I write it sits before me on my study table, the final proof to me of Kirsten's story. What I found was a curve of brass with a blue stone set in its midst. The pin is broken, but it shines as clearly as the day Sandy handed it to Kirsten on the beach by Plocaig. It reminded her of a beach, it reminded me of every detail of her story.